A Name of Honor

BY Kathleen McAlpin Blasi

ILLUSTRATIONS BY Leslie Bowman

For Grandma, who showed me a new path, and
for Mom, who traveled it with me
—K.M.B.

To my mother, my first teacher
—L.B.

Text copyright © 2007 by Kathleen McAlpin Blasi
Illustrations copyright © 2007 by Leslie Bowman under exclusive license to MONDO Publishing
All rights reserved.
No part of this publication may be reproduced, except in the case of quotation for articles
or reviews, or stored in any retrieval system, or transmitted in any form or by any means, electronic,
mechanical, photocopying, recording, or otherwise, without written permission from the publisher.
For information contact: MONDO Publishing, 980 Avenue of the Americas, New York, NY 10018

Visit our website at http://www.mondopub.com
Printed in USA
07 08 09 10 11 9 8 7 6 5 4 3 2 1
ISBN 1-59336-692-2
Designed by E. Friedman

Library of Congress Cataloging-in-Publication Data
Blasi, Kathleen McAlpin.
A name of honor / by Kathleen McAlpin Blasi; illustrated by Leslie Bowman.
p. cm.
Summary: A young girl growing up in Sicily in the early 1900's longs to
fulfill her father's dream for his family and seek a new life in America.
ISBN 1-59336-692-2
[1. Names, Personal—Fiction. 2. Family life--Italy--Sicily--Fiction. 3.
Emigration and immigration--Fiction. 4. Sicily
(Italy)—History—1870-1945—Fiction.] I. Bowman, Leslie W., ill. II.
Title.
PZ7.B61362 Na 2006
[Fic]–dc22

Contents

Acknowledgments

The seed that sprouted to form this story came from my mother, Gloria Giofrida McAlpin and her memories of her mother (my grandmother), Gaetana Curatolo Giofrida. Thanks, Mom.

Although the historical accuracy of this work is ultimately my responsibility, I extend my thanks to: Jeffrey S. Dosick and Barry Moreno, Library Technicians, Ellis Island/Statue of Liberty National Monument; Josh Graml, Researcher, The Mariners' Museum Research Library and Archives, Newport News, Virginia; Gaspare (Gap) Mangione; and Alan Unsworth, Reference Librarian, Rush Rhees Library, University of Rochester. Special thanks to my friends in Sicily: Francesco (Ciccio) Di Caro, Carmelo Guardione, Vincenzo Ricotta, and Calogero Vilardo.

Many wonderful books helped me to learn about and to understand the immigration experience and the Sicilian/Italian culture: Ships of Our Ancestors *by Michael J. Anuta;* Island of Hope/Island of Tears *by David*

M. Brownstone, Irene M. Franck, and Douglass Brownstone; From Sicily to Elizabeth Street *by Donna R. Gabaccia;* A Pictorial History of Immigration *by Oscar Handlin;* If Your Name Was Changed at Ellis Island *by Ellen Levine;* Mount Allegro and America Is Also Italian *by Gerlando (Jerre) Mangione;* Time-Life Books' Immigrants: The New Americans; *and* Italian Immigrants: 1880-1920 *by Anne M. Todd.*

Thank you to those who reviewed A Name of Honor *at various stages of its development: Debra Braun, Brian Burley, Robin Halladay, Lynne Madden, MaryAnn McAlpin, Steven J. McAlpin, Dan Osborn, Carol Pembroke, Beth Ann Walck, and the Burley/Osborn Bookclub (Max Banaszak, Marie Blasi, Jay Fleckenstein, Michelle Hart, Elisabeth Montemorano, Kathryn Sprague, and Adria Wiedrich). Heartfelt thanks to my critique colleagues, who constantly raise the bar: Andrea Page, Jennifer Meagher, and Jamie Moran, and to all the members of Rochester Area Children's Writers & Illustrators for their willingness to share their knowledge, experience, and love of the field.*

Special thanks to my friends at Mondo Publishing, with whom I am honored to publish my first book: Lainee Cohen, Susan Eddy, Mark Vineis, and Devorah Grosser.

Finally thank you to my families—the McAlpins and the Blasis—for your encouragement and enthusiasm, especially to my brother, Michael, who fueled the ember that is my love of writing and to my father, Frank McAlpin, who instilled in me the entrepreneurial spirit necessary to make a go of this writing business. Immeasurable thanks to my faithful cheerleaders—my husband Frank and my children, Meg and Marie. Thanks for believing.

CHAPTER ONE

Home

Rochester, New York, 1985

"So, Grandma, are you going to Sicily with us, or what?" my ten-year-old granddaughter asks.

"Or what," I reply with a smirk.

"Grandma!"

"I can't go back to the old country, honey. I'm sorry."

"Why? Give me one good reason."

Feeling as if I'm teetering on a tightrope, I stir my tomato sauce, carefully forming my answer. It's Sunday—"Sauce Day" in our family. I make it. They come from miles around to eat it. In this regard, I won't let them down. And I will do almost anything for my grandchildren. But I will not make this trip. "The long plane ride, the ship, all that walking. See? Three good reasons." I pat her hand.

"But it's Sicily! We'll see where you grew up, your father's church, your home . . . ."

I hold up my hand for her to stop. I close my eyes. *Home.* Sicily was a place to *spend* one's life, not to *live* it. My childhood consisted of working hard until my fingers bled in order to fulfill Papa's dream of leaving our homeland. And my granddaughter wants me to go back? "No, dear. *Remembering* Sicily is enough for me. You go ahead without me. When you return, I'll be right here, ready to make Sunday sauce for you again." I wink at her to mask the heaviness in my heart.

She smiles halfheartedly and sighs. I know she's disappointed. She doesn't understand. But maybe it's time that she did.

"Wait here," I tell her. "I need to get something."

I return with a small wooden box and place it on the table. The lid creaks when I open it; there, lying on top, is the fragile blue fabric, milky with age. With my special sewing shears, I cut a perfect square and place it in my granddaughter's hand, like a frail, wounded bird.

"What's this?" she asks.

"I want you to take it to Sicily with you."

"Why?"

I push the box aside, and its splintered edge catches on the tablecloth. How careless I am! Such a special cloth. I pull it taut, and the loose thread stretches back into place. Shall I start there—with the story of the tablecloth?

I study my granddaughter's face. Funny how long lashes, a turned-up nose, or a birthmark connects one generation to another. "Our family's past is part of you, little one. And you are the future of our family. But one can't look forward without first looking back."

CHAPTER TWO

The Cursed One

Serradifalco, Sicily, Italy, 1912

I was eight years old the day I learned that my name was cursed. While my 12-year-old sister, Lucia, swept the floor, I cleaned the table. Rather than brush the meal's remains into my hand, I let them spill onto the floor to make her job more challenging. She caught me.

"Gaetana, you! *You* are named after dead people!" Lucia taunted, her voice dripping with revenge.

"We are all named after dead people, Lucia," I answered uneasily.

"No, Gaetana. It is more than that. Mamma and Papa tried your name on two dead babies before they gave it to you!"

Now, my people are not renowned for creativity when it comes to naming babies. Giuseppe, my older brother, was named after Papa's father. Lucia, whose name danced off the tongue, was named after

Mamma's mother and her favorite saint. My younger brother, Antonino, honored my father. My name's roots, too, were found in Papa's side of the family tree, which I much preferred to my mother's stern side. Thus I was named Gaetana, for Papa's mother—or so I was led to believe for the first eight years of my life.

I stared at Lucia. My mouth hung open in disbelief. Named after two dead babies? My pride in being named for Papa's mother withered like a dying leaf.

"Lucia!" Mamma shook her fist at my sister. "A child does not need to know such things!"

"It is true then, Mamma? Papa?" I had been tempted to brush this off as one of Lucia's crazy outbursts.

"Let me explain," said Papa gently. "As you know, my mother's name was Gaetana. It is tradition to name children after one's parents. It is honorable. After Lucia, another baby girl was born to our family. We named her Gaetana. She lived only…ten minutes."

I gulped.

"Our next baby," Papa continued, "also a girl whom we named Gaetana, was sick and died before she was . . . two months old."

I gasped.

Papa rubbed his thumb over the back of my hand. He smiled.

"Then you came along. Finally my mother's namesake. You see?"

I saw that I helped Papa gain the status of "the good son," giving him a way to carry on his mother's name. I already knew that names dictated the course of one's life. My own sister, Lucia, whose name meant "light," was afraid of the dark. Indeed, names were telling!

My mind raced to make a list of the bad things that had happened in my life thus far:

10

1. Nearly choking when as a toddler
   I put Mamma's sewing needle in my mouth
2. Toppling over the loft stairs, where the
   broom stabbed me in the side
3. Having Lucia for a sister

With dread I awaited the day my fate would befall me with full force. Would I live to be Mamma's age? Lucia's, even? There had to be a way for an eight-year-old girl to shake her impending doom.

When I awoke the next morning, I descended the loft stairs. Mamma sat in the rocking chair in the hearth room, the largest of the three rooms in our house. Her hair, as usual, was twisted in a neat bun. I wondered what time she got out of bed to achieve such perfection. Never had I seen hair as black as my mother's—so black that in the sun, it appeared almost purple. I stood before her. *You can do it, Gaetana!*

Mamma rocked back and forth as she sewed the blanket for the baby growing inside her. *Squeak. Thud. Squeak. Thud.* Each time the chair rocked forward, her skirt momentarily rested underneath the rocking chair's runners. And each time she pushed back, her skirt flew, just in time, from underneath them. I stood there watching, mesmerized.

"Gaetana?" Mamma interrupted my reverie.

"I . . . I want to ask you something." I took a deep breath to muster my courage. "Mamma, I would like a new name, please."

"You say this as if you ask for a drink of water or a slice of bread. What is wrong with you?"

"Nothing is wrong with me. Not yet anyway. Mamma, please! I must change my name!"

Mamma stopped sewing, looked me squarely in the eye, and replied, "You have always been 'Gaetana,' and 'Gaetana' you will always be." She poked her needle through the fabric and pulled it towards her.

"But my name does not suit me. It is too long. I am a short girl. I need a short name." I bent my knees slightly to hide the fact that my skirt no longer touched the floor.

"Of course you are short, Gaetana, as are most eight-year-old children."

"But, Mamma, if I had a short name, think of how quickly you could call me when I am trouble! *If* I am trouble . . ."

Silence.

"Ta could be my little name," I suggested.

"*Ta* is not your name."

"But Nino is short for Antonino," I reasoned. Nino was my three-year-old brother.

Nino, hearing his name, ran to Mamma and clambered up into her lap. She set down her work and folded him in her arms. I saw an opportunity.

"Neeee-noooo," I sang, "can you say, 'Ta?' Come, Nino. Say 'Ta!'"

"T . . ."

"No! He will not say 'Ta,'" Mamma thundered, "because that is not your name! 'Gaetana' is the name Papa and I gave to you—"

"—and two dead babies!" I cut her off, hands on my hips.

Mamma's full lap and swollen belly did not stop her hand from meeting my cheek with stinging force. "You will respect your grandmother and our two precious babies who look down on us from heaven. Not another word!"

Papa, who had not been feeling well and was getting a late start, entered the room. He looked as tired and weak as he did the day before. "Luigia, she is just a child—"

"—who does not know when to give up! Not a very attractive trait in a girl, I might add!" Mamma was on her feet now, and Nino on the floor.

"Luigia, do not raise your voice to me!"

"Antonino," my mother pleaded, "she talks of changing her name. Crazy!" Mamma waved her hands wildly in the air.

Papa gently pulled Mamma to the corner of the hearth room and whispered what I hoped to be recommended leniency. His hand gently rested on her large belly. Mamma stared silently at the floor and nodded. My eyes wandered, wanting to focus on anything but my parents' exchange. Giuseppe and Lucia peered from the loft, my sister grinning. I scowled at her. My predicament was, after all, her fault.

"Gaetana." It was my turn with Papa now. "You will not speak to your mother with such disrespect."

"But, Papa, my name is bad luck. Two babies died—Lucia told me, and . . ."

"Your mother will deal with Lucia," Papa said, nodding toward Mamma. I noticed only one pair of eyes now spying from the loft. He continued, "Nonna would not be pleased if her granddaughter changed her name. Remember that it is for *her* you are named— someone who was brave and true and kind." His voice became raspy,

like mine did when I tried not to cry. He bowed his head. After a moment, his voice became strong again. "You have a beautiful, honorable name. And someday you might even come to *like* it, Gaetana. Imagine that!"

"Yes, Papa. Imagine that." I had nearly made my father cry. This man, who worked so hard as the custodian of the church, who played with me on Sundays, yet who could make me shiver with a mere glance. How could I disrespect him so?

"I must go now, Gaetana. Work, work, work until we have enough money to leave Sicily. Do you know that in America, I will work half as hard and earn twice the money?"

"Yes, Papa." I had heard this many times. Since I was a very little girl, Papa had talked of leaving Sicily. It all started four years earlier, in 1908, when the earth opened up and swallowed the Sicilian town of Messina. Within minutes a wave taller than my house swept over that town, killing those who remained. Papa had told Mamma that Providence was speaking loud and clear—that it was time to prepare to leave our homeland.

"But this is our home, Antonino!" Mamma had cried.

"Are we to stay in a place that is plagued with disaster, where we are uncertain of our next meal, simply because it is home? No, Luigia. A better life waits for us in America."

◆◆◆

"We will be late! Come, Giuseppe!" Papa called to my 15-year-old brother.

Giuseppe scrambled down the rickety stairs with an eagerness that was absent from Papa. *Today Papa looks as if he is about to end his day rather than to begin it.*

"Ready, Papa!" answered Giuseppe. "Ready to be a man, just like you!" He patted my head, and with a wink, he was gone. *Lucky Giuseppe!* Like most peasant children his age, he no longer attended school. He helped Papa in the church and Papa's brother, Zio Angelo, in the fields to earn money to add to the chest my parents kept under their bed. I couldn't wait until I was old enough to help earn money for my family—money that was needed to feed and clothe us and ultimately to travel to America.

I was grateful that Papa wanted to take us to a better place, and I loved him with my whole heart. And I knew he loved me. Yet he didn't understand me. No matter what Papa said, I was still the one named after two dead babies. How could he expect me to ever like my name when I would have to dodge its looming curse for the rest of my life?

CHAPTER THREE

The Water Fountain

"Gaetana, hurry along, and get the morning water," ordered Mamma.

"Yes," I answered. This was one of my regular chores.

"After school you will help me to wash the clothes as well," she said.

"But that is Lucia's chore."

"And today it is yours."

I knew better than to ask why. I stepped outside into the beating sun, walked down the few steps leading from our door, and picked up the water jug. Glittery spiderwebs were draped from one side to the other. *Oh, if only I were brave enough to catch one to put in Lucia's hair!* I tried to brush the webs away, and a whole army of the creatures marched over my fingers. I screamed and dropped the jug. Mamma appeared in the doorway in an instant.

"Careful, Gaetana! You will break it. Hurry now, or you will be late for school!"

I lifted the jug and moved out of Mamma's sight. *Careful, Gaetana,* she'd said. Gaetana. *Ugh. If only I could change my name! If one of the baby Gaetanas had lived, I would be a Maria or maybe a Margherita. Would I be forced to disrespect Mamma? No! Would I have to wash the clothes? No! Would spiders attack me? No!*

I had a shaky, sick feeling in my stomach. I knew I would feel better later though, when school and work were done and we would gather here in the street. I would laugh with my brothers, sister, and neighbors while the adults talked and played matchmaker. Maybe Papa would tell us one of his funny stories. But for now, the chores (and Mamma) would not wait.

Each day on my way to the water fountain in Piazza San Francesco, I passed the same people doing the same things in the same sand-colored streets and buildings of my little neighborhood. Today was no different. Beyond these streets, distant houses were tucked into hillsides, their dark windows peeking out like curious eyes. I walked on, dreaming of Sicily's rolling hills and the possibilities that lay beyond them. And somewhere past those hills was the great city of Palermo, where, Zio Angelo had told us many times, life moved along at a dizzying pace.

The water fountain allowed me to be the most informed in my family. While I awaited my turn, I learned from the other girls and women what was happening in our small town. They talked of who was marrying whom, who had died, and who was leaving for America. This last subject always piqued my interest, since someday my family would be the subject of such talk. Oftentimes families did not go to America together. At the water fountain, I witnessed the tears of those left behind—wives, children, and mothers—separated from their loved ones for months or even years. Being the informer of the Curatolo family gave me status—if only for a brief few minutes—upon my return from the fountain. But there was a price.

On my water-gathering trips, I chanced running into Mamma's sister, Zia Teresa. For reasons I didn't understand, Zia Teresa and Mamma had been angry with one another for years. This was even more baffling because Zia Teresa was married to Zio Angelo, Papa's brother.

We children were not allowed to speak to our aunt, an extension of the silence that hung between her and Mamma. On this day, my aunt lurked about the water fountain like a troll. A girl I recognized from school stood beside her—a girl Lucia had warned me to stay away from.

Zia Teresa cleared her throat. "Wait your turn, Santina," she said to the girl. "You will then fill the bucket and walk home."

"Yes, Mamma."

Santina was my cousin! I inched toward the fountain. Oh, how I wanted to talk with her! I filled my water jug, balanced it on my head, and raced home, breathless and sweaty, the sloshing water soaking my hair.

"Mamma, did you know I have a cousin named Santina?"

"Yes."

"I see her at school, and Lucia does not let me talk to her!"

"I am glad to hear Lucia follows my orders. You will, as well."

"But she is family, Mamma!"

"She is the daughter of a nasty woman who is supposed to be my sister."

"Mamma . . ."

"Off to school. Lucia is waiting for you in the piazza."

I turned toward the door. My sister. That *snake*. If only I had had the courage to keep a spider for her. I could have put it down her blouse or on her head. . . .

"Gaetana, have you nothing to say to me?" asked Mamma.

I looked into her expectant black eyes and swallowed. "I am sorry, Mamma. I will try to be good."

"You have a stubborn streak. It will not serve you well to let your tongue run free, Gaetana."

"Yes, Mamma." I left my house to continue my daily routine. Little did I know that my life was about to change in ways I never imagined.

CHAPTER FOUR

Papa

The next day, when the morning sun had not yet brightened the sky, Papa kissed the tip of my nose. I hadn't heard him creep up the stairs, which he did every morning, to say goodbye to Lucia and me. We slept on the floor on a large straw mat. I was lucky to have the end spot, so Papa's morning kiss could easily reach me.

"Where are you going?" I asked foggily.

Papa spoke softly. "I am going to work at church today, Gaetana, just like I did yesterday and the day before that."

Papa tousled my already messy tresses. "Now *that* is beautiful hair!" He laughed. "Perhaps word of this new style will reach Palermo, and all the rich ladies will want to look just like Gaetana Curatolo!" Papa's teasing was a sure sign he forgave me for yesterday's outburst. I hugged him, then held him at arm's length to study his face. Dark circles hung beneath his eyes, and his skin was the color of the dry, dusty street outside our window. His hand held tightly to his chest.

"Papa, what is wrong?" I asked.

He shrugged. "I am not feeling quite like myself today. It must be Mamma's cooking." He held a finger to his lips and winked.

"Papa, please do not work today." He was working too hard. Not only did he take care of the church, but sometimes he also helped Zio Angelo work the fields. And whenever a neighbor needed help, Papa was the first to volunteer. Mamma often complained that if Papa weren't so generous, perhaps our own roof would be patched and our table sturdy.

"I must work today, Gaetana. How else will we ever have enough money to go to America? I will be home this evening, and we will gather in the street, as always."

"But you are supposed to help Signor Rosa fix the wheel on his cart," I reminded him.

"Oh, yes. Well, right after that I will come home."

"Papa, I want to work with you, like Giuseppe does." Someday I would not have to go to school anymore. But it wouldn't be to help Papa. All that Sicilian parents wanted for their daughters was for them to marry Sicilian boys, for whom they would cook, clean, and sew. The sooner they practiced, the better. Working with my father sounded much better to me.

Papa lowered his voice. "If you come with me, you could not go to school, and I would have to answer to your mother. We would not want that, would we?" His voice was strained, and again I was struck by how tired he looked, although his workday had not yet begun. He stretched over me to kiss Lucia.

"Goodbye, Papa," Lucia yawned, brushing her hair from her forehead. Papa kissed me again and was gone. I scratched my cheek where his whiskers had tickled me.

After school that day, I wiped the table. Mamma liked it cleaned before and after we ate. Our tiny house was so hot that in between visits to the cooking pot, Mamma lingered in the doorway to grab what little relief the late day offered. A light breeze lifted her hair. She wiped her forehead with the back of her hand. The sun began to leave its pink mark in the sky—it was getting late.

"Where are Papa and Giuseppe?" My voice seemed to wake Mamma from a daydream.

"Hmmmm?" She glanced up the street and smoothed her hair, although it was already plastered to her head. "Working, of course. Have you wiped the table? I told you to wipe the table, Gaetana."

"I did, Mamma. Remember? You handed the cloth to me, and . . ."

"Do it again! And then make certain Nino is not pestering the neighbors."

"Lucia is watching him."

"Just do as I say!"

"Yes, Mamma."

Why is Mamma so grouchy? If the baby in her belly is the cause, then I will never have one! I wiped the clean table and went to the street, where I found my brother and his friend playing catch with a rock. Nino was about to throw it at our neighbor, Signora Rosa, when I heard frantic running. I turned to see Giuseppe racing towards us. He was alone.

"Mamma!" he screamed, his face flushed.

Mamma scurried down the steps and ran to meet my brother. "Giuseppe, what is wrong?" she asked, clutching his shoulders. A

23

crease between her eyebrows formed, deep and dark.

"Mamma," my brother moaned, not bothering to wipe the tears from his face, "we worked all day. He did not look well. He rested. He said he was fine. But he just grabbed his chest and fell to the floor! I tried to help him. It happened so fast!"

"Oh!" Mamma wailed. "Oh, no. No!" Mamma dropped to her knees and doubled over, as if she were going to vomit.

What happened fast? Where is Papa? This morning he was pale, and now he is sick.

"We must get him, Mamma," I stated, hardly believing this wasn't obvious to her. "We can make him better. Come, Mamma!" I cried. Mamma buried her face in her hands.

"Come with me, Giuseppe. We can help Papa come back here."

Giuseppe shook his head. He sank to the ground, resting on one knee, eye level with me. "Gaetana, Papa is not coming back. I am so sorry. Papa . . . is . . . gone."

"What? Where? Did he go to America without us?"

"Oh, I do not want to say this! Gaetana . . . Papa is dead."

Dead? Papa dead? How can this be? He is not old! But I already knew that even babies could die. Giuseppe's mouth moved, but his words floated away. For a moment, I imagined he was Papa, kneeling before me, assuring me that everything would be all right. But this was not Papa. *This is Giuseppe.* I pushed him and started running. *I will see the lie for myself. How can my brother say such things? Mamma will punish him!*

The church was just around the corner. There was a group of men. I ran past them but suddenly couldn't move. I finally spun around to see Papa's blurry face staring at me, tear-stained and ruddy. "Papa!"

"Gaetana, it is me—Zio Angelo. Gaetana, please, come." He held out his arms and crushed me in his embrace. No, this was not Papa. He didn't even smell like Papa. The tears came then, in a torrent that I thought would never end.

"What is happening, Zio? Why?"

"Gaetana, I am sorry. So sorry. My brother, your papa . . ."

"Please, Zio. Please tell me he is *not* . . ."

"Oh, if I could. I saw him myself, love. Your papa is happy in heaven now. We are sad to live without him. But I will take care of you."

"I will take care of you, too, Gaetana." It was Giuseppe. "And Mamma, and Lucia, and Nino, and the baby." His voice lowered with each name he spoke. He ran his hands over the prickly hair on his face, as if he was washing it. I didn't want Giuseppe to take care of me. *No one can do it like Papa.*

"Come back to the house, Gaetana," begged Giuseppe.

I looked at my uncle. Zio Angelo nodded and took my hand. When we returned to Mamma, I realized that I had never before seen a truly sad face. I stepped toward her, sobbing, as the truth of this day became hauntingly clear. What was left of my family huddled in the street. Nino tugged on Mamma's skirt, begging for something to eat. Even Zia Teresa was there, hovering nearby. She took a step toward us and whispered to her husband, "I will get the black cloth."

"No!" Mamma cried. "This cannot happen! My Antonino. . . ." She let out an anguished cry, and I held my hands over my ears until the worst of it was over.

I rubbed the back of my hand under my nose and sniffed, remembering Papa's kiss from that morning. I looked down the street at the still darkness. *Maybe this is just a terrible mistake.* But Papa was not there. *Was this my fault?* I had had bad thoughts about my name. I had nagged Mamma. *Oh! I am sorry, Papa!* My stomach twisted.

"Come in the house, Gaetana," Giuseppe urged. I followed my brother over the threshold. The crying and wailing were even louder in the confined space. I took a deep breath. The sweaty smell that filled the air when Papa came home was not there. But all these people were. In my house. Papa's house. *Go away!* I ran to the bedroom and grabbed Papa's nightshirt off the bed. Holding it tightly, I buried my face in it. *His smell!* How long would it last? Forever? My heart, which used to leap at the sight of Papa, quivered in its emptiness.

Papa had grabbed at his chest. *If his heart was weak to begin with . . . did I break it when I lost my temper with Mamma and make his frail heart give way? Or did my curse find its way to him, taking him from us?* I rubbed my throbbing forehead as I considered these bleak possibilities.

Somewhere in the dark, children laughed and squealed. *Don't they know my Papa is gone?* I wished I did not know. *I will never laugh again. And I will never go to America.* Not without Papa. I will stay in Sicily, where I can be near him always. I lay down on my parents' bed and pulled my knees to my chest. I don't remember falling asleep, but when I awoke, I felt Papa's nightshirt beneath my cheek, its dampness reminding me that the images coming to me were not a nightmare. I touched my cheek and almost felt Papa's scratchy whiskers against my face. I thought of the baby Gaetanas in heaven—the lucky ones who were with Papa now.

CHAPTER FIVE

Changes

The black cloth hung in our doorway to let the world know that Antonino Curatolo had left it. Mamma said he was in a better place. I knew that must be true because anywhere would be better than my home without my father. He was laid out on Mamma's bed for a day so that family and friends could pay their respects.

No matter how many times I looked at him, part of me refused to believe that this was Papa. His hair meandered all over his head, and I tried to smooth it. *Perhaps word of this new style . . .* A sob caught in my throat. I touched his arm. *Wake up!* I dragged my fingers across his cold skin, and they seemed to stick. I drew a sharp breath and pulled my hand away, but not before Mamma caught me.

"Gaetana! What are you doing?"

"Mamma, what if we put him in the ground, and he is not really . . ."

"I know it is hard to believe." Her shoulders shook, and her hands covered her face.

I went to Mamma then and put my arms around her. Her hands dropped from her face to my shoulders. I drew her closer to me. But the moment was over. Her hands returned to her eyes to catch her grief. *Let them fall and touch me again. Papa cannot touch me, but Mamma can—if she wants to.*

I let go of my mother and turned again toward my father. "Papa, I love you," I whispered. "I am sorry for when I made you angry. I will try to be good!" Giuseppe came to my side. He put his fingers under my chin and gently tilted my head upward. His face mirrored mine. *Is this boy really the man of our house now?* I softly dabbed his eyes with my black sleeve. With Papa gone, this was to be the color my family would wear—I for the next 10 years, and Mamma for the rest of her life.

To help ease our pain at Papa's loss, we did what most Sicilians did in their time of great need. Every day we made our dark procession to the church to light a candle in Papa's memory. I felt a fleeting comfort, being in a place so important to Papa, a place he loved. But an overwhelming sadness pushed the comfort away. Evidence of Papa was everywhere I looked—the dustless pews, the neatly stacked prayer books, the perfectly repaired windows. Now this was to be Giuseppe's church. He would carry on for Papa.

My baby sister, Mia Curatolo, came into the world two months after Papa had left it. When I was sad, I reminded myself that at least I could always remember Papa. Little Mia would never know our father—would never see his teasing smile or hold his gentle, callused hand. *I will love my baby sister even more because Papa cannot.*

By this time, Lucia and I had quit school to help Mamma sew and

care for the little ones. As much as I had loathed my lessons, they were easier than sewing clothes and chasing Nino all day. I learned something very important when I was forced to leave school: A person cannot truly miss something until she does not have it anymore. By the time she understands it was something good, it is too late.

At times I got angry with Papa for leaving us, for changing our lives. And sometimes I could not help but wonder what our lives would be like if only I was not cursed, if only my name was something that brought good fortune. Mamma said that it was God's will that our lives had taken this turn. At first she viewed Papa's death as a sign that we were not meant to live in America. But conditions in Sicily were getting worse. The landowners from the north paid southern Sicilian laborers little. These laborers, in turn, could not readily pay Mamma for the clothes we made. Working hard to get nowhere was not the way of life my father had wanted for us. Mamma decided to honor Papa by keeping his American dream alive.

"We must work and save our money, however long it takes," she said. "Someday America will be our home."

"We will not have to work in America?" I asked hopefully.

"Only I will work, in a place where they make fancy clothes for rich people. We will eat big meals together, and you will go to school. Like a dream come true. Papa's dream."

Three years later, in 1915, Giuseppe followed his own dream and married Caterina Calo, the shoemaker's daughter.

"Mamma, how will we get along without Giuseppe?" I asked.

"Giuseppe is right next door, Gaetana."

No matter what Mamma said, I missed my brother! Since Papa

had died, I had looked out the doorway at the same time each day, waiting to see Giuseppe stroll toward home. Now that he was married, I still watched each day and was both relieved and saddened when he passed, pausing barely long enough to brush my cheek with a light kiss. How could Mamma possibly think it was the same?

Giuseppe—like Mamma, Lucia, and me—continued to work hard and save, but our dream of living in the Golden Land would have to wait. In 1915, much of the world was at war. Some of the families in our town traveled to the seaport of Palermo to catch a ship to America, only to be turned away and forced back to Serradifalco. The Atlantic Ocean was speckled with warships, and some ports were closed, making travel to America very difficult.

One day Zio Angelo returned from Palermo. I loved to see him after his trips to the city, for he would bring us bigger news than our little town's water fountain could ever provide. On this day, he showed up at our door without his usual playful expression. The creases around his eyes seemed deeper, and he didn't pinch my cheek (as he usually did) in greeting.

He pulled Mamma aside. "Luigia, the news from Palermo is not good today. It seems Italy will certainly enter the war. Soon."

"No, Angelo!"

"Yes. You must leave now, before the waters are closed off completely. I do not wish to see you go, Luigia, but I know it is in your heart, as it was in my brother's heart."

"I cannot go now! There is not enough money for all of us to go." Mamma's face turned ashen. "Giuseppe. Oh, no. My son! If Italy goes to war . . ."

"He will have to serve."

CHAPTER SIX

The First to Leave

Giuseppe paced the hearth room and rubbed his chin. "Mamma, how can I leave my family? Papa would be ashamed!"

"My son, if you stay here, you will have to fight in the war. If you fight, I'm afraid you will die. I will not lose you, too!" She held his face in her hands. "I would rather give you to America than give you to the war."

"Mamma, you need me to take care of you."

"Zio Angelo will help us. Go. It is the right thing to do. I am certain Papa would agree."

I didn't agree. It was bad enough having my brother move from our house. Now he was to move from our country! Still, like Mamma, I'd rather have Giuseppe move to America than die in battle.

The evening before Giuseppe and Caterina were to leave, we gathered in the street. They exchanged a curious look.

"Go on, Giuseppe. Tell your mother," Caterina coaxed.

"Tell me what?" asked Mamma.

"You tell her," urged Giuseppe.

Mamma looked from one to the other. "You torture me with your secret!"

"Mamma," Giuseppe began, "you are going to have a grandbaby." Since my brother's wedding, Mamma often talked of the grandchild that would someday call her "Nonna." And I was to be Zia Gaetana! An aunt at the age of 12! It sounded so grand and made me feel very grown up. I loved it—at least the "zia" part.

"Oh, Giuseppe!" Mamma exclaimed. "That is wonderful! A baby!" She turned to Caterina. "Oh, but for you to travel in your condition . . ."

Giuseppe stepped in front of Caterina. "Mamma, if we stay . . ."

"No, Giuseppe. You must go. I will see my grandbaby someday soon." Mamma's words hung in the air like a fog. *Someday? When we have enough money and the war ends? How long will that be? Will their baby still be a baby?* Mamma took Giuseppe's and Caterina's hands in hers. "Papa would be proud."

"If the child is a boy, he will be Papa's namesake."

"My grandbaby." Mamma drew a deep breath, silent for a moment. "We will work harder, so that we can see my grandbaby— sooner rather than later!"

Giuseppe held Mamma close. "I will send money. Save it with your earnings. I promise we will be together in no time at all."

The next morning my uncle's cart wobbled down the bumpy street, taking my brother from Serradifalco. I feared that "together" was something my family would never be again.

◆◆◆

Nearly two months passed before Mamma complained that her son had not written her. But at last, it happened, and one would have thought that the biggest news out of Palermo had landed right on the Curatolo doorstep.

I held the wrinkled envelope, hoping for its contents to bring a smile to Mamma's face. "A letter from Giuseppe!" I announced.

"Finally! Oh, give it to me!" She turned the envelope over in her trembling hands. "What if their voyage did not go well? Oh, and the baby. Poor Caterina—perhaps she was too frail."

"Please, Mamma!"

"Yes." She took a deep breath. "Where shall we read it? By the hearth? Or . . ."

"Mamma!" I was about to snatch the envelope from her and read it myself. Finally, she sat in the rocking chair, straightened her hair, and smoothed her skirt.

"Mamma?"

"What?"

"Giuseppe cannot see you."

"Yes, yes. Get the others, Gaetana. They will want to hear their brother's news. Hurry!"

Lucia, Nino, and Mia scrambled into the house, and we sat at Mamma's feet. She tore open the envelope and pulled out the letter. A smile slowly formed.

> Dear Mamma, Lucia, Gaetana, Nino, and Mia,
>
> Writing all those names is a painful reminder of all that Caterina and I leave behind.
>
> We arrived! The crossing was hard on Caterina, but she is well now.

The baby begins to change her shape. I will be very happy to become a father but am uncertain that New York City is the best place to raise my family—so different from Serradifalco! Gone are the green hills of my homeland and the air that makes one want to take a deep breath.

I have work at a construction company, but there is word that the new foreman despises Italians. He cheats them of their wages.

Here is some money, Mamma. I hope you are well and that Zio Angelo looks after you. I pray I did the right thing.

Love,
Giuseppe and Caterina

Each time Zio Angelo returned from Palermo with news of the war, I knew my brother had done the right thing. Italy entered World War I shortly after Giuseppe left, and travel to America came to a standstill. Had he waited, he would have been stuck on the wrong side of the ocean, forced to serve in the Italian army.

Six months later, my favorite letter arrived.

Little Antonino is here! He is a perfect, healthy boy, with Papa's chin and Caterina's eyes. He saves his first smile for Nonna.
Here is more money for your chest, Mamma. I know why you made me leave. I will protect my boy, no matter his age.

When you get to America, you will need to travel a bit further than New York City. An Italian worker from the construction company told me that Rochester, New York, is the place to be. Now I have work, peace, quiet, green, and more money in my pocket. Many from Sicily are here, too. All that is missing is you.

Little Antonino sends his love.

Mamma ran to her bedroom and picked up the blanket she had made for the baby. She held it to her face and sniffed deeply. "I will make a blue one now. A baby boy needs a blue blanket, do you not think so, Gaetana?" *Mamma asking for my thoughts? This baby makes Mamma happy. Oh, I love this baby!*

News of the latest Curatolo propelled me to the water fountain that day. Since Santina now made these trips alone, we sometimes met in secret. I considered making a big announcement about my nephew, but decided instead to share my news privately with my cousin. Waiting in line, I caught her eye and scratched my nose. This was our signal to meet behind the shoemaker's shop. We couldn't risk talking at the fountain, for fear our mothers would find out.

"Santina! Giuseppe and Caterina had a baby boy!"

"This is the very thing we need to bring our mothers together. I will tell Mamma, and she will make amends with Zia Luigia!" Santina kissed the tips of her fingers. "Perfect!"

"How will you tell her you know?"

"Silly girl," Santina answered. "Did you not hear all the women at the water fountain talking about the new baby?" She winked.

"No . . . oh, right!" I smiled. My clever cousin.

But news of her great-nephew failed to bring Zia Teresa to our doorstep, and Mamma didn't seem to care. The joy she derived from the birth of Little Antonino was sustained by the birth of his little brother, Carlo, in 1917. Mamma's grandchildren gave her an odd combination of happiness and sadness. One day I overheard her say to Zio Angelo, "It is almost torture knowing I walk this Earth with my grandsons and cannot see them. I am happy that they are in our family. But they are not in my life."

I, too, was anxious to hold my nephews in my arms. But I would have to wait. The war raged on until 1918, when I was almost 15 years old. We cried upon hearing the news that the fighting had ended. We could have a new beginning.

"The war is over! The war is over!" six-year-old Mia squealed. She paused. "What does that mean, Mamma?"

"It means our family can be together again. It means we are one step closer."

CHAPTER SEVEN
A Good Match

1918

"Mamma, are we going to the piazza today?" Lucia asked.

"You went there yesterday!" I exclaimed. Lately Lucia had one thing on her mind. Boys. Mamma brought her to the piazza and paraded her around until one of them would have *her* on *his* mind.

"Take care of yourself, Gaetana!" said Lucia, hands on her hips. "The more Mamma takes me to the piazza, the quicker I will find a husband. Someday it will be your turn."

"I will never shop for a husband." *Like you.*

When they returned from the piazza, both Mamma and Lucia were flushed with excitement. Dante DeNunzio, the mason's son, had asked Mamma's permission to court Lucia. Now all Lucia talked about was Dante, Dante, Dante. It was enough to turn my stomach!

After only one meeting, Mamma and Dante's mother concluded

that their children made a superb match. Within a year, my sister was engaged to be married.

"After the wedding, Lucia and Dante will travel with us to America," Mamma told me, Nino, and Mia. Knowing her eldest daughter would begin her new life nearby caused Mamma to do strange things, like hum as she dusted and reprimand Nino in an almost sing-song voice.

We were eating our evening meal when Mamma's mood shifted like a Mediterranean wind.

"Dante's uncle has work for him in America," announced Lucia.

"Wonderful! You will be set when you go there, unlike your brother, who had to look for work while taking care of his expectant wife."

"Dante is leaving *now*," Lucia explained. "His uncle can hold the job for him only a short time. Dante will send money to me for my passage. When I get to America, I will live with Giuseppe until the wedding. . . . " Her voice trailed off.

"You will get married in America?" I asked.

"Gaetana, I am talking to *Mamma*. You have something to say about every little thing!"

"I would say this is a *big* thing." I turned to my mother.

Mamma set down her spoon as if it were a delicate egg. "Lucia, the wedding will not take place here in Sicily, with your family?"

"No, Mamma." Lucia seemed to be conversing with her soup rather than with Mamma.

"Then you will wait for us."

"No."

"You will get married without your family?" Mamma asked.

Silence from my sister.

"Lucia?"

"I am sorry, Mamma. That is the way Dante wants it to be."

"I do not like this. And you should not, either. For a time, you will be here, and he will be there. Unmarried. Far from the eyes, far from the heart."

"What else can I do?" she asked helplessly.

"I will tell you what else you can do. Tell that lying . . ."

"Mamma!" cried Lucia.

"Oh, he tells me he will take care of you. Of us! But is it true? No. He makes you travel alone across the ocean! And he will marry you without your family to witness!"

"Giuseppe and Caterina will be there. And my new family—his family—will witness."

"It is not enough."

"Dante is to be my husband. I must respect his wishes. Surely you understand this!"

"Your father would never have had me marry without my family's blessing."

"Mamma, Dante is not Papa. . . ."

"Clearly!"

"Oh," said Lucia, exasperated, "there is nothing I can do!"

"You tell him no!"

"No to my future husband? Then I will have no husband at all! And I will stay with you until I am an old woman!"

Mamma paused from her tirade. I looked from her to Lucia and back again, waiting for someone to speak.

"That is it, then. You will make him happy at the expense of your family. Yes. Go, Lucia. Marry in America. One less passage for me to pay." She stood and began to clear the table.

Lucia's forehead sank to the table, where she sat for the next hour and cried. I considered putting my arm around her to comfort her.

Instead, I helped Mamma clean the dishes.

Less than six months later, we stood in the hearth room, preparing for Lucia's departure. My family was falling apart before my very eyes. First Papa, then Giuseppe and Caterina, and now Lucia. With each goodbye, Mamma offered fewer smiles and became more stern. Vague images of my mother's smile laced my thoughts. Was it the way Mamma *used* to be or the way I *wanted* her to be?

"A wedding without the mother," Mamma lamented. "What would Papa think?"

"Do not worry, Mamma," I said. "We will be together again soon, and our family will be even bigger, with Giuseppe's boys and Dante . . . and, oh, Mamma! Maybe Lucia will have a baby, too!" Mamma put her face in her hands and cried. Defeated, I slumped against the hearth.

Lucia poked her head in. "Gaetana, now look what you have done!" She ran to Mamma and stroked her hair.

"What *I* have done?" I asked with disbelief. "If you were not so selfish . . ."

Mamma stood. "Stop. Please. Not today."

"Sorry, Mamma," said Lucia and I in chorus.

Lucia looked about the hearth room. "Nothing more to pack. I suppose I am ready."

"No, you are not." Mamma wiped her eyes and hurried to the

bedroom. She returned with the gift she and I had worked on many nights, long after the rest of the family had gone to sleep: Lucia's wedding dress

"Oh, Mamma! Gaetana! It is beautiful!" The fabric spilled through her fingers. "I wish you could come to America. I wish you could be at my wedding! I wish . . ." Lucia's lower lip trembled, and tears spilled from her eyes.

Mamma hugged my sister. "Look ahead now. Do not wish for what will not be. Our hands made this with love, Lucia. On your wedding day, you will wear the love of your family."

Lucia hugged Mamma tightly and then took a step toward me. "Thank you, Gaetana."

Our dark eyes met. I ran my fingertips along her cheek, as if I were seeing her for the very first time. Her eyes told me she was feeling the same way, and when we embraced, I did not want her to go. Her touch warmed me inside like nothing else had in a long, long time.

CHAPTER EIGHT

Mario

"We should have heard from Lucia by now!" groaned Mamma.

"Giuseppe's letter arrived 61 days after he left," I recalled.

"You counted?"

"Yes," I admitted. "How many days since Lucia left, Mamma?"

"Hmmm . . . 58, if you include today."

"I see you count, too."

At last it came—Lucia's first letter from America.

My dear family,

It is wonderful here, but it feels strange to be without you.

Dante and I have decided to wait, as rushing a wedding cannot bring good luck. Please hurry!

I keep busy helping Giuseppe and Caterina in their lovely house and with the boys. Little Antonino never stops talking and moving, like Nino when he was small. And Carlo is starting to walk (waddle).

Caterina teaches me to cook many things. And I will cook for you, too. No more soup! Think of all these things during your crossing. You will need to remember why you take such a difficult journey.

The sea was rough and the sleeping quarters dark and eerie. As your voyage progresses, so will a horrible smell. Each night I prayed the next day would come quickly so that I could escape the darkness and return to the deck to breathe fresh air again.

After ten days, you will see something amazing! The Statue of Liberty stands tall and proud. She is more beautiful than I imagined.

I was scared at Ellis Island, Mamma. The men in charge shout orders. The different languages confuse. A woman from Messina was taken from her family because she was sick. They would not let her enter America. Her husband and children wept, and the officers did not care!

Be well.

All my love,

Lucia ("Lucy" in America)

"She is safe! Thank God!" Wide-eyed, Mamma scooped me in her arms and hugged me so tightly that I held my breath, as if its release would break the spell of her fleeting happiness. I did not want to let go of her.

As if struck by a sudden realization, she waved the letter in the air. "Humph! Lucy!"

"I wonder what my American name will be." *Perhaps I will not have to live with my cursed name forever!*

"American name? You are Italian, as is your sister, no matter what they call her. I will write her and remind her of this."

There were other things I wanted to remind her of—like how my list of chores grew upon her leaving. With Lucia gone, in addition to fetching the water and helping Mamma sew, I also prepared our evening meals. With each stir of the soup, I imagined my sister sitting in a fluffy chair, sipping tea, and eating pastry. Eventually, though, my resentment turned to gratitude.

One day, as I approached the water fountain, I heard mumblings of my name. When the water gatherers saw me, they became suddenly silent and enthralled with the fine detail of their buckets. *They are talking about me!* I gave Santina the nose-itching signal, and we met behind the shoemaker's shop.

"Tell me what they say about me!" I demanded.

"Gaetana, have you bought bread lately?" Santina asked with a grin.

I felt the blood race to my cheeks. "Bread? Who does not eat bread, at least occasionally?" I crossed my arms in front of me.

"But who buys the bread, Gaetana? Your Mamma? Or do you buy the bread from Maaaaario?" It took her a full three seconds to pronounce the first syllable of the breadmaker's son.

My frown was quickly replaced with a smile. Talk of Mario and me was my favorite topic of conversation. And to think that we were deemed worthy news for the water fountain!

Santina continued. "Mario's sister told us that his favorite time of day is when he comes to your house to sell bread."

"*Favorite* time of day? Did she use that very word, Santina?"

She nodded eagerly.

I certainly knew the reason he felt this way, but nevertheless I loved hearing it. Mario's selling bread had become my favorite time of day as well. "Santina, did Mario's sister say anything else?" I asked.

"Hmmm . . . she did say something about her mother raising the price of the bread. . . . "

"You tease me, Santina! Mario is so—well—so handsome and nice. Do you think he feels the same way about me?"

"Well, it would seem odd for him to think of you as handsome," Santina answered, "and as for nice, he never saw you argue with Lucia!"

I laughed so hard that I almost knocked over my bucket.

"Oh, Gaetana, I laugh with no one like I laugh with you. Cousins who cannot see each other openly! It is crazy!"

I nodded. "If only we did not have to sneak around. We could walk down the street and hold hands."

"Yes, if only. Now I must get back with the water, or Mamma will wonder what took me so long. Goodbye, Gaetana."

"Goodbye, Santina."

I watched my cousin turn the corner. *Mario likes me. That is good.* Things had been going along well for some time now. Did my name curse die with Papa? Or was it lying in wait for me to be happy, only to steal my joy like a thief?

The next day, Mamma said matter-of-factly, "Gaetana, I have good news for you. It is time to lighten your burden a bit."

This is too good to be true! No more cooking? No more sewing? We are giving Nino away?

"Mia is old enough now for the water chore. Today I would like you to show her how."

Panic set in. "No, Mamma. Mia is much too young for such responsibility. No, no. I will do it."

Mamma set her hands on her wide hips. "Gaetana, how old is Mia?"

Surely, she knows how old her children are! Has my curse affected her brain? "Mia is eight, Mamma."

"And how old were *you* when you began to fetch the water?"

"Eight," I whispered.

"Show your sister how to fetch the water, Gaetana."

"Yes, Mamma."

Mia had a lot to learn in terms of water fountain reporting. When she returned from her first solo trip, I quizzed her. "Did you see a girl with thick, straight hair and a mole on her cheek, Mia?" I asked.

"Yes."

"Good. You know the bread boy—Mario?"

"Yes."

"That girl is Mario's sister!"

Silence.

"What did she talk about today?" I prodded.

She shrugged her shoulders. "She wore a pretty dress and a ribbon in her hair the same color. I wonder if I could have a ribbon like that? It was blue! Just like the sky, Gaetana!"

"Oh, Mia," I sighed.

Nonetheless, Mario's daily visits continued for months—a good sign, I was sure. Eventually Mamma limited our bread-buying to twice a week in order that we might save more money.

"He is a good boy," said Mamma of Mario, "a boy who someday would make a good husband."

Although Mamma approved of Mario, I was not allowed to break long from my chores to talk with him, and I was not permitted to be alone with him. Mamma had told me many times, "Proper young ladies stay true to their tasks, no matter how handsome the distraction might be!" So Mario and I talked briefly in the street, where Mamma (and the entire town) could see us.

One evening as I stirred the soup, I looked up to see Mario walking toward my house. *It is Tuesday—not a bread day for us.* He held his mother's freshly made bread in the air. As he passed our doorway, he beckoned, with a wave of his hand. I glanced over my shoulder. Mamma was nowhere in sight. I slipped out quietly, my heart pounding like Mamma's voice in my ears.

I followed Mario around the corner.

"Gaetana!" Mamma called. "Where are you?" I didn't answer. For Mario to lead me from my house, he must have something important to say. But what?

"Gaetana," Mario began, "our mothers have spoken. It seems they believe us to be well-suited, but there is one problem."

"Yes, Mario. I know. I cannot marry before my older sister. And Lucia will not marry until we go to America!"

"That is why I wanted to see you today. I have something to tell you." He paused. "My father's bakery is doing well in America." The bakery was in Rochester, New York, where my brother and sister lived.

"That is good!"

"He sent my family enough money to join him there."

What? Now Mario, too? I pressed my fingers together and raised them to my lips.

"Gaetana!" Mamma's voice was getting closer.

"It has been three years since I have seen Papa," Mario lamented. "I cannot deny that I will be happy to see my father again, Gaetana. But to leave you . . ."

My eyes stung, and I became aware of the tears that had dropped to my hands. I wiped them on my skirt. "Family is important, Mario. You must go." *And the further you are from me, the better! What if my curse has already touched you? Will you make it safely to America?*

"Say what you are thinking, Gaetana."

He would not understand. "I will miss you, Mario." I reached up to touch his gritty, stubbled face.

He took my hands and held them to his heart. "I will wait for you. I shall marry you someday, my Gaetana. That is a promise." He kissed my hands and let them fall. I said a silent prayer for his safety. Then he was gone. The wheels of his cart stirred the street dust, making it rise and float softly behind him.

"There you are!" It was Mamma. "What on Earth are you doing?"

My eyes remained fixed on his silhouette. "Everyone leaves, Mamma. Even Mario."

CHAPTER NINE

The Girl With No Hands

Nino waved an envelope in front of my face. "Gaetana, look what I have!" He swooped it behind his back.

"Who is it from? Nino!"

"Instead, I will tell you who it is *not* from. Giuseppe. Lucia."

"A letter from Mario! Give it to me, Nino!"

He took a step towards the door, but didn't get far before I grabbed him by the trousers and plucked the envelope from his clenched fingers.

> *Dear Gaetana,*
> *America! You will love it here.*
> *He is safe!*
> *I see your brother and sister, as we live near them.*
> *Papa's business keeps me very busy, but it is work that does not break one's back—or one's spirit. With the money I earn, we eat meat and bread*

nearly every day—like kings! But this king is nothing without his queen. I look forward to news of your arrival, Gaetana. Will I recognize you?

I smile thinking of you.

Mario

No more? Anxiously, I turned the letter over, looked in the envelope, and wondered whether a page was missing. I was certain Mario had traveled steerage, like Giuseppe and Lucia, but he made no mention of the crossing, the ship, the food. Nothing! I said a silent prayer of thanks that ship conditions had improved since my brother and sister had traveled.

The year 1920 brought many things—more money for Mamma's chest, news from America, and our growing desire to live there. The letters described an easier life, with happy people. Hoping America would have the same effect on Mamma, I couldn't wait to get there. Would America make me happy, too?

My hope for this new life was also peppered with the sadness of remembering my childhood, with a Papa to see each morning and each night—a time when I was unaware of fate's cruelty. Reminders were everywhere. In Mamma's sad eyes. In Papa's nightshirt, which I kept under my pillow. In the voices of children running down the street to school. I would have gladly traded places with any of them—to have a father. These thoughts formed a stubborn lump in my throat.

Then came the day I discovered a welcome respite from my gloom. I had left my scarf in church, and Mamma sent me back to get it. To no avail, I looked in our seat and on the floor. I spotted a girl kneeling near the front of the church. I weighed the rudeness of interrupting a person in prayer against the foolishness of coming home empty-handed. The decision was easy.

Afraid that I might startle the girl, I approached with noisy footsteps that echoed from the marble floor to the ornate ceiling. Her chin hung to her chest. Her arms were crossed in front of her, and draped over them was my scarf.

"Excuse me," I said. "I see you have found my scarf." I held out my hands to her.

"This belongs to you? Oh, I admire the stitching. Did you make it?"

"Yes."

"It is beautiful." She stood. Her eyes, level with mine, were almost black, her lashes so long they nearly touched her eyebrows. Who was this beautiful stranger? Why had I never before seen her?

She extended her arms toward me. I lifted the scarf. "Thank . . ." I stopped in horror. My eyes darted to her face. Long ago the girl with no hands had been the talk of the water fountain. The villagers' comments ran through my head like a runaway cart. *The shame! What use will she be to her family?*

She stared, unblinking, as if expecting something. I couldn't speak.

"I was born this way," she offered.

"I am sorry. I did not mean to stare. I have never seen . . ."

"Sorry?" she asked, her eyebrows arched high.

"I did not mean to be rude. My . . . my name is Gaetana."

"And I am Ida."

"I have never seen you, Ida. Serradifalco is such a small town, you would think I would recognize you—at least from when I used to go to school."

"I have never been to school. My parents thought it best to keep me home. I help my Mamma sew—nothing as fine as this, of course."

"Sew?" I asked, leaning in. *Did I hear her correctly?*

"Yes."

"But . . . how?"

"With my feet. It is a wonder what you can do when you don't have all of your parts." An infectious smile stretched across her face. "You have been to school, no?"

Of course she wants to change the subject. "When I was young."

"Do you know how to read?" she asked, as if she was afraid of the answer.

"Yes."

"How I wish I could read! I know that a book could take me away from Serradifalco, if only for a moment. What an escape that would be!"

An image flashed before me, Ida and I sitting quietly, a book between us. "I can teach you to read! As long as I complete my chores. What do you think of that?"

"You would do that for me? Oh, yes. Yes! I would like that very much!"

"Ida, I must tell you. My family is saving money to go to America. We might leave soon. I do not know."

"Then let us get started!" she answered, a giggle bubbling in her voice.

◆◆◆

"Read," Mamma encouraged. "Teaching Ida will help you, too." Mamma saw my teaching Ida as a chance to improve my reading skills.

She knew what America expected of her new arrivals. By the time we traveled, we would be required to pass a literacy test in order to enter the country.

Teaching Ida to read became the one thing I looked forward to. Up to this point in my life, all I did was for the good of the family and myself. Ida helped me to discover the joy of helping someone else.

One day I confessed to Ida that I had a dream that Mario was to marry a giddy American girl with yellow hair and blue eyes. I was certain my dream was a bad sign.

"From what you have told me many, many, many . . ."

"I see your point, Ida. I talk too much of Mario!"

". . . times," she continued, "Mario is a man of honor, Ta. He will wait for you. Dreams mean nothing, you silly, superstitious girl!" When Mamma was not within hearing, Ida called me "Ta," the non-Gaetana name I had longed for since my childhood.

"But what if he did, Ida? All those American girls . . ."

Mamma entered the room with a bundle of laundry. "You know what they say, Gaetana. Far from the eyes, far from the heart."

"Mamma, Mario waits for me."

"It is simply one of the Sicilian truths. He goes to America. The girls there are different. He meets one. He likes her. You are here. . . ."

"But he said he would wait!" I pursed my lips, holding captive the words that slammed against the inside of my mouth. *Sicilian truth. Soon that will not matter anymore. We will be American. Gaetana Curatolo—the American girl.* Something seemed amiss.

Mamma left the room to continue her chores.

"What if Mamma is right?" I sighed.

"Oh, if only I could wring your neck!" We laughed until tears streamed from our eyes.

"Ida, I will miss you so! Perhaps your parents will change their minds about staying in Serradifalco."

"Never. They will not leave the home of their ancestors. They will wait for things to get better."

Ida's parents would hang on to a generations-old tradition at any price. It made me wonder how my family could so easily forsake the honoring of tradition. Or was it that easy?

CHAPTER TEN

Keepsakes

June 1920

When our life-changing letter from Giuseppe arrived, Mamma opened the envelope and stared. Then she walked to her bedroom as if in a daze. I heard the familiar sound of the chest sliding out from underneath the bed. *Poor Mamma! When will there be enough money to make her dream come true?* But this time, she gasped, "Children, come quickly!"

We crowded the doorway and saw Mamma standing at the foot of the bed, money falling through her quivering fingers and into the chest. "Giuseppe has sent more money than ever before!" Her voice quavered, as if she wasn't sure whether to laugh or cry. "At last we have enough! *Arrivederci*, Serradifalco! We're going to America!"

Several weeks later, we were ready to bid our homeland farewell.

"Gaetana," Mamma said, "for ten minutes you have dusted that table!"

"I am sorry. My mind wandered."

"Well, make it wander back to this house, which must be cleaned before we leave. And hurry. Zio Angelo is kind enough to take us to our ship. We will not keep him waiting."

"Yes, Mamma." I watched the dust float and sparkle in the spotlight of early sun streaming through the open door. Like one of those specks, my emotions were wandering aimlessly. On the one hand, I looked forward to our new life with our family. On the other, I dreaded saying goodbye to those I would never see again.

Eight-year-old Mia came down the loft stairs, her blouse bulging. "I am ready to go to America!" She lowered her arms, and her favorite rocks and sticks fell to the floor.

"What is this?" Mamma asked impatiently.

"This is what I am taking to America."

"No. We must leave these here, Mia. We have so little room in the chest."

Mia pouted silently, too young to understand the packing priorities, but old enough to know not to argue with Mamma.

I waited until the others had left for the piazza before I took one last walk through our tiny house. It was difficult to imagine someone else living here, but at least it was family—Mamma's cousin would move in.

With one last glance into Mamma's room, I caught sight of Papa's nightshirt. *What is that doing in here? I know I put it in the chest!* I picked up the shirt and held it to my face. *No room in the chest,* Mamma had told Mia. I quickly tucked it under my skirt, between my waistband and underclothes.

"Gaetana, come!" Nino called. "Mamma is looking for you."

"I will, Nino. I just need a moment."

"For what?"

Could an 11-year-old boy understand? "I need to say goodbye—in my own way."

He shrugged his shoulders, shook his head, and walked out the door.

I stepped outside. Everything was right where it belonged—except for me, it seemed. The sturdy buildings lined my street, as they had for as long as I could remember. And the water jug lay where it always had, at the bottom of the steps by the washtub. Here, in this familiar street, my family and neighbors had gathered many times over the years. Papa had entertained us with his stories. Here, I had first learned of Giuseppe's upcoming wedding—and then of his baby. I squeezed my eyes shut to burn these images forever in my mind.

I plodded along the street and paused between two buildings. There was a perfect view of the countryside—another image I would take with me. Later the village men would emerge from the quiet fields to return from their day's work. Another day that fathers would share meals with their wives, sons, and daughters. My throat tightened and ached, but I moved on.

I reached the piazza, where a crowd had gathered to bid farewell to the Curatolo family.

"Ta—Gaetana! There you are! I have something for you."

"Ida!"

My best friend stood before me, a cloth draped over her arm. She raised it toward me. "For you."

I held the cloth above my head, its silken threads catching on my fingers' rough skin. As it unfolded in a rolling cascade of tiny, perfectly arranged squares, I knew who had made this tablecloth. I threw my arms around my friend. "It is beautiful! Thank you!"

"You bring it to America, and think of me when you use it."

I turned to my mother. The storage chest lay on the ground near her feet. I knew it was filled to the top with the things Mamma decided were important—clothes, food, and our traveling papers. There was no room for a tablecloth, and there was no room under my skirt either.

"Mamma, look what Ida made for me! Now I have something to remember her always!"

Mamma looked from the tablecloth to Ida to the chest. Kneeling, I opened the chest and pushed the cloth into it. It didn't fit! I pushed down hard, but still the chest wouldn't close.

Mamma squeezed my hand. "There is no room in the chest for a tablecloth." She turned to my friend. "I am sorry, Ida."

Ida closed her eyes for a moment and nodded. "Gaetana, I will keep it for you. Someday when I see you again, you will have it."

I knew that someday would never come. "No!" I turned to my mother. "I must take it with me. Ida worked so hard, for so long, just for me." I glanced at the chest. "Mamma, we can leave some of my clothes here. I do not need all of them."

"But I only brought a few things!"

"Oh, Mamma, as long as I have extra underclothes. . . . When we get to America, we can make more clothes. Please, Mamma!"

She sighed. "Very well."

"Thank you, Mamma!" I rummaged through the chest, replacing my clothes with this precious gift.

I stared at Ida, willing myself to remember every detail of her face. I couldn't imagine my life without her. The words I wanted to say stuck in my throat.

"Gaetana, you will shine in America. I know it," said Ida. "You are going to be great!"

I hugged my dear friend, and my words found their way. "*You already are.*"

CHAPTER ELEVEN

Farewell

Zio Angelo reached into his cart. "Before we go, Luigia, I have something to give to you." He gently lay palm branches in Mamma's hands. "Teresa asked me to give these to you. My wife wishes blessings on your American home."

"Then she should have brought them herself." Mamma thrust the palms toward my uncle.

"I tried. That is all I can say. I tried, and . . . " Zio Angelo's eyes wandered and suddenly stopped. His lips formed a pursed smile.

Mamma whirled around. "What . . . ?"

Zia Teresa! Mamma's hands flew to her mouth and then out toward her sister. The two women ran to each other, tears spilling from their eyes.

"Luigia, we have wasted so much time!"

"Please forgive me," Mamma begged.

"And you have forgiven me?"

"Yes," Mamma croaked.

I watched the reunion unfold. I looked to Zio Angelo to make sure I was not dreaming. He stared, laughing and crying at the same time. It was then that I noticed Santina standing beside him. I ran to her, and we fell into an eager embrace. The piazza became silent, and we looked back to see Mamma and Zia Teresa watching us, wide-eyed.

"You two . . . " Mamma began.

" . . . know one another," Zia Teresa finished.

"How?" asked Mamma.

"When?" asked Zia Teresa.

"We saw each other at the water fountain when we were little," I explained. "We knew we were cousins, because I saw her with you."

"We met behind the shoemaker's shop once."

"Or twice," I added.

"Our daughters are wiser than we are, Luigia. We have missed so much!" She grasped Mamma's hands. "Are you certain you want to go to America? Angelo tells me the stories of its wonders are not true, that they tell tales only to lure people."

"No, Teresa! My children's letters would not lie. We are going. You can, too."

"Our life is here and always will be."

"I suppose what is right for one person is not right for another," Mamma conceded.

Nino and Mia had joined Santina and me. Zia Teresa beamed. "Ah, your children are beautiful, Luigia." I saw an invitation to run to her. I peeked over my shoulder, happy to see Mamma's approval. She watched with a smile that made the butterflies in my belly dance. It was the first time I had ever hugged my aunt. And it would be the last.

Zio Angelo patted his shirt pocket. An envelope, which held our steamship tickets, poked out of it. He had purchased them on his last trip to Palermo. "I have dreamed of this day—my wife and my brother's wife together again—but I am afraid that it is time to go."

Mamma, Nino, Mia, and Santina joined our embrace. I tightened my arms around Zia Teresa, holding a promise renewed that family stood by one another, no matter what. And I held the regret that this part of my family would have to live only in my heart from now on. Like Papa.

The cart lurched forward. I looked back to watch the Piazza San Francesco and those I loved there shrink in the distance. "Mamma, look! See them? Still, they wave!" Mamma looked briefly and jerked her head forward again. She stared straight ahead, her shoulders rigid. *How can she not care? Or maybe she cares so much that she cannot bear to look.*

Familiarity, even when laced with misery, is comforting. I left a world of hunger and hard work—a world of late nights spent sewing until my fingers bled, a world of caring for my young brother and sister and of cooking for an entire family what looked to be barely enough for one person. Still, this was the only world I had ever known. My world.

The cart rambled over the craggy road. Thoughts of Mario, Ida, the family we left behind, the steamship, and my family in America danced in my head. *Will we ever come back? Is Mario still waiting for me? Will Americans be kind or cruel? Will I fit in?* The rickety yet steady movement of the cart lulled me to sleep.

When the cart stopped suddenly, I awoke. "Where are we, Zio?"

"We have reached a good place to spend the night."

"Is this someone's house?" I asked. "Do you know them?"

"Not really. This is a place that was built for travelers, so they have a place to rest. It is not fancy, but it puts a roof over our heads."

We slept on the floor that night, among others on the same type of journey. Somehow this floor, unlike ours in Serradifalco, made it difficult to sleep. I got up and tiptoed to the window. My stomach turned, and a memory stirred. I had felt something similar when Papa died. But this was different. Every fear I had ever felt in my life came rushing to me at once. With my heart slamming in my chest and sweat collecting in my palms, I buried my face in my hands and cried.

CHAPTER TWELVE

Palermo

I cannot see a thing, but somehow I know it's Papa's church. I rub my eyes. Far away a light appears. "Gaetana," he calls. My mouth silently forms his name. The light moves closer. It's a candle, but why is it floating toward me? A shadow. Who is holding the candle? Papa? The flame is so close that its heat spreads over my face.

"Papa!"

"Gaetana, it's me—Zio! Wake up!"

My eyes were mere slits, and the sun poured in, warm across my face. "Oh, it is you."

"If only my wife were so happy to see me, too," he quipped.

"Sorry, Zio," I yawned. "You know I love you, but even you cannot compete with a dream of Papa." My neck and back ached from the unfamiliar sleeping arrangement. Even though the hour was early, a sweaty film already covered my face.

We traveled all day through the base of the mountains, winding our way to Palermo. The sun was just beginning to sink as we entered the great city. Zio Angelo had told us of this place, but to see it for myself was something else. Never in my life had I left my little village; here I stood in a city that floated on the sea. We passed a building with precise angles and tall, grated, arched windows. A stone wall with a fence surrounded it. It looked to be the home of a king.

"Who lives there, Zio Angelo?" I asked.

"That is the opera house, Gaetana. Wealthy people go there to listen to heartbreaking stories set to music. I hear it is quite lovely."

Someday I will see the opera.

We walked on. Vendors crowded the streets, shouting to sell their wares.

"Fresh fish here!"

"Buy one! Get another for half the price!"

Pushcarts overflowed with seafood, greens, and shaped breads whose aroma made my stomach rumble. *Maybe Mario will have his own pushcart in America!* Buckets like the one I had used to hold water in Serradifalco spilled over with colorful flowers. People rushed along the cobblestone paths, stopping here and there to peruse the city's offerings.

Although many people were dressed plainly, like us, a parade of fashion passed before my eyes. Men tipped fancy caps as they greeted passersby. Women were colorful in layered, ruffled skirts that swooshed as they walked. How I longed to wear something other than the black of my father's death! It would be two more years before I might dress like these fine ladies.

A man walked toward us, a big smile on his face, his hand

extended. *Zio Angelo has friends everywhere.* The man spun around. His gleaming shoes made a perfect circle in the dirt. A pipe bounced from the corner of his mouth as he spoke. "Do you see what you can have if you come to America?   I will help you get tickets. New clothes, too. Come, old man," he said to my uncle. "I am sure I can find a job for a fellow like you."

"Oh, how nice . . . " Mamma began.

"No!   Not nice, Luigia," warned Zio Angelo. "Stay away from people like him." He turned toward the man. "We do not need you—we have our tickets. Go on, now!   Find someone else to sell your lies to."

"That is fine," said the stranger. "if you want to look like greenhorns." He walked away laughing and scanned the crowd.

Mamma, her eyebrows furrowed, shook her head. "He was only trying to help, Angelo. Once we do not have you to take care of us, who will we have? No one!"

"There are very few people you can trust here, Luigia. They use you, try to make you spend more money than you have. Trust me. I hear the stories."

Nino touched the top of his head. "What is a greenhorn, Zio? Do I look like one?"

"No, Nino. It is what they call newcomers who do not know American ways. It is cruel."

We continued on to the dock. "Here we are!" declared Zio. "Luigia, come with me to make sure everything is in order. Gaetana, stay here with the children."

The sea glistened, casting rays of light onto the city's tall buildings.

How I longed for the chance to see what was inside them! Nino discovered how to toss rocks in the water, and Mia and I soon joined in. Our game ended abruptly when an elderly woman warned us that it was not safe to play near the water. *Unsafe? And we are to travel across it to America?* We backed up from the dock and spent the next hour watching ships arrive and depart. Their human cargo looked both happy and sad. *How will I look when it is my turn?*

Mamma returned, waving papers in the air. "Children! We are set. But the ship will not come until tomorrow." She looked around uneasily. "We will make the best of it."

"I will stay with you until you leave, Luigia," offered Zio Angelo.

Mamma gently touched my uncle's arm. "No. We will stay in the dormitory. Go home to my sister."

"I will not leave you in this strange place. How will you take care of yourself and the children?"

"Angelo," Mamma laughed, "once you go home, I will have to care for my family. Or have you forgotten that you will not escort us all the way to America?"

"And have you forgotten about the man of the family?" asked Nino, standing on his toes.

"You will be the man of the family when I am gone. Now, Luigia, not another word." Zio held a finger to his lips, just like Papa on the last morning I saw him. "I have a friend who lives here in town. He and his wife would be happy to welcome us for the night."

Zio Angelo's friend, Tonio, and his wife, Tia, fussed over us like we were royalty—starving royalty.

"You want more cheese, Nino? How about you, Gaetana?"

"No, thank you," I said for the twentieth time. My belly was so full, I feared my waistband might burst, revealing Papa's nightshirt.

"Very well," said Tia. "Some bread then?"

This continued until Mamma, fearing we would leave them with nothing to eat, offered to give them the sausage and bread she had packed in the trunk.

"You must save that for your journey, Luigia," said Tonio. "From what we hear, I imagine it is better than the food provided on the ship."

After supper we settled in to sleep. Tia stood in the doorway and shook her head. "My sons have married and left me. I am so happy to have you here. Good night."

Zio Angelo tossed about on the hard floor at the foot of the bed.

"Are you sure you are all right down there, Zio?" I asked.

"Of course!" he said, as he continued to flip-flop from side to side. "Discomfort builds character, and I could use a little more!" I heard a flash of my father in his teasing voice. *Oh, I will miss my uncle! Will I forget Papa without these reminders?*

I pressed my fingers into the soft bedding and watched it spring back. It was so unlike my old bed that I couldn't sleep. And the noise! In Serradifalco, it was so quiet you could hear your neighbors talk in their sleep. But here I heard men shout and laugh. Doors slammed. The clock struck, and I counted. Eleven chimes. With envy I listened to my brother's and sister's rhythmic breathing.

In the morning, our ship had not yet arrived, but there was plenty to do in preparation. The officials had to check our traveling papers, which proved who we were and that we had not broken the law. They also needed to check our bodies to make sure we were free of disease.

This is a day I will never forget.

"Mamma, no. I do not want anyone to see me!"

"Gaetana, everyone must do it."

I squeezed my eyes shut, as if by not being able to see anyone, they couldn't see me, either. I could feel the heat on my face and neck. I quickly rolled Papa's shirt inside my skirt. The inspector handed our clothes to another woman, who took them away. She poked through my hair and checked my mouth. Then she checked my eyes with a hook-like tool. Oh, the pain! I knew from Zio Angelo that she was checking for the eye disease trachoma. He had told us that some people in Sicily got trachoma from drinking bad water. *What if we have the disease?* She shooed us on.

I crossed my arms over my chest. I heard a familiar sound, like rain on our roof at home. *But wasn't it sunny when we entered the building? Where did the storm come from?* We entered another room, where water sprayed from holes in the ceiling above.

I remembered Lucia's letter. Water poured down over me. How strange and wonderful! It felt good after the hot, dusty journey from Serradifalco. When we were through, a matron handed my clothes to me. I quickly put them on, carefully placing Papa's shirt back in its secret spot. The clothes smelled different—clean but harsh.

"Mamma, ours must be a clean ship," I said as I buttoned my blouse. "Like Mario's." Mario's letter mentioned nothing of his voyage, unlike Lucia's with its brief yet not-so-pleasant description of the sleeping quarters.

"What do you mean?" Mamma pulled her scarf down under her chin and tied it.

"They want us clean to keep the ship clean."

"Do not raise your hopes, Gaetana. It means only that they do not want the ship made dirtier by dirty people."

"Still, it could be a very clean ship . . . . "

She didn't answer.

CHAPTER THIRTEEN

The *Patria*

Mamma handed my ticket to me. "Do not lose it," she warned. The number 21 stood out boldly, larger than any other writing on the ticket. *Gaetana Curatolo – Number 21.* Looking closer, I could hardly believe my eyes. Our ship's name was the *Patria*, meaning "fatherland". I held the ticket for my uncle to see. "Look, Zio! Papa is with us." I scrunched my eyes to keep my tears inside.

"Of course, he is," said Zio Angelo.

The sun's rays pounded our black clothing, which grew damp with sweat. We inched our way toward the rear of the ship. Like Lucia and Giuseppe, we were to travel steerage—the least expensive way to reach America. Two shorter lines of passengers headed for the vessel as well—one toward the middle of the ship and one toward the front. The people there had umbrellas to protect themselves from the sun and trunks so large that I was certain everything we had owned could have fit into one of them.

Mia cried, "Hold me!"

"It is too hot," said Mamma. She stroked Mia's wet hair.

"My legs hurt," whined Mia. "My feet hurt. Please, Mamma!"

I felt badly for my little sister, but would feel worse for all of us if Mamma lost her patience. "Sit down on the trunk, Mia, and take off your shoes," I suggested. "I will rub your feet. But you will have to stand when it is time to move along."

We neared the gangway. "Well," said Mamma, "it is time for one last goodbye. Thank you, Angelo." Mamma clung to Zio Angelo so long, I thought there would not be time for me. She stepped back and wiped her eyes. It was my turn.

"Bless you, Gaetana. Have a safe journey, and please write to us."

I kissed his weathered hands. Such a good man, taking us to Palermo, staying with us until it was time to leave. I wished I could have more time with him to make up for when Mamma's and Zia Teresa's feud kept our families apart. I knew that if given the chance, I could discover even more of my father in him.

"I will think of you every day," I choked. "Please tell Santina the same."

The massive *Patria* loomed before me. *How can something so big and so heavy stay afloat? What if a tidal wave—like the one that swept over Messina—rises up and swallows us, too?* The dread I had felt en route to Palermo returned tenfold.

Nino read my thoughts. "Mamma, what if the ship sinks, and . . ."

"Shhh! Keep your comments to yourself, Nino. You will scare the others."

We crept along the gangway at the rear of the ship. Mamma held

Mia's hand. Nino and I carried the trunk. Closer and closer to steerage, and closer to understanding Giuseppe's and Lucia's letters. Again I wondered why Mario's letters had said nothing about the bleak accommodations.

Once on board, we planted ourselves near the deck railing, where the breeze could find us and we could find Zio Angelo on the dock. Many others crammed into the center of the deck, waiting restlessly in the heat as the remaining passengers boarded.

Finally, as the *Patria* moved away from the dock, a breeze caressed our faces. "*Ciao*, Zio Angelo!" I called. He waved his hat to us and wiped his eyes. We waved, too, as my uncle gradually blended in with the other specks on the dock. Before long, the mountains surrounding Palermo looked like a thick, jagged line floating on the water. Black smoke spewed from big pipes on the ship and drifted toward us. I turned to focus on the one advantage to traveling at the back of the ship—the best and longest view of the life we had left behind.

"Pull your scarves over your heads, girls," Mamma instructed us. "We need to keep our hair clean." Steeped in tradition, Mamma had kept her scarf on since we had left our home.

Elbows on the railing and chin in my hands, I watched the foamy water below. Blue and green swells formed a steady wake that raced the ship. The *Patria* sliced through the water at surprising speed. *Surely, it will not take ten days to reach America!* I tapped into the arithmetic I had learned in school. The trip to Palermo was about 50 miles. Our journey across the ocean to America would be over 4,000 miles. The numbers fell into place, and I shivered.

"Gaetana, are you sick?" asked Nino. His voice startled me. He had been unusually quiet on board, as if hypnotized by the churning sea.

Perhaps this voyage would not be so bad after all!

"No. Why do you ask?"

"You shake as if you are cold."

"Mamma, Gaetana is sick!" proclaimed Mia.

"I am not sick!"

"Maybe we should find some water for you," Mamma offered.

"I am fine, Mamma. Please!"

Mia's thoughts shifted quickly. "Mamma, will there be a water fountain in America? Will that be my chore? I want to get the water, Mamma, just like in Serradifalco."

"That won't be necessary. The water will be in our home."

"Will everything be different in America?"

"Many things will, but the important things stay the same—our family, our traditions." Mamma wrapped my sister in her arms, and I secretly wished that I were the one there. *I still need you, Mamma.* I rested my hands on Mia's shoulders and kissed the top of her steamy head.

Mamma tugged at my sleeve. "Gaetana, come with me down below. The children are hungry and tired."

Hand in hand, we formed a Curatolo train as Mamma led us down a dark, narrow staircase. By the time we reached the bottom, my eyes adjusted to the scant light. The fresh salty air from the deck above was not permitted here, and I took a halting breath. The smell was not as bad as Lucia had said, but then our voyage had just begun.

Nino urgently pulled on Mamma's sleeve.

"What is it, Nino?" she sighed.

"Look! The men and boys go there!" he cried, pointing in the opposite direction.

"No, Nino. You are a young boy and will stay with us. You will not sleep alone."

Mamma took us to a tiny cabin. Beds barely wide enough to hold an adult were piled one on top of the other. Mia's whining grew to a full-scale moan.

"Stop fussing, Mia," Nino urged. "Crying will not make it better." He turned toward Mamma. "You see? It is good I can stay here with you."

"Yes, I agree. I do not need two children who fuss!"

"Two? I do not fuss!" Nino argued.

"Then who was that boy on the brink of tears when he thought he must sleep alone?"

"You do not understand, Mamma. I was only afraid to leave you and the girls alone."

"Of course, Nino. You think of us—as the man of the family should." She tousled his hair, and he scowled at her.

We placed the chest at the foot of one of the bunks. I smoothed the sheets on each musty, stained mattress. But that wasn't good enough for Mamma. "I will not lie my head where countless others have." She opened the chest. "We will sleep on our extra clothes." I, of course, had forfeited mine for Ida's gift. Mamma handed the tablecloth to me.

"No, Mamma. How can I?" Ida meant for the cloth to adorn my table someday—not to serve as a bedsheet.

Mamma looked from the mattress to me. "How can you not?"

Resigned, I spread the cloth over the pillow.

The shipping company provided food, but this night we ate a little piece of Serradifalco—Mamma's bread and sausage. There was nothing to do after we ate but go to bed. I assumed sleep would come easily, but I was wrong. The thick, moist air made it difficult to breathe, and the engines pounded their sad, steady song. But eventually my body gave in to my exhaustion.

◆◆◆

I awoke with a start, expecting to see my sister and brother beside me, tucked in the corner of the loft in Serradifalco. Then I remembered.

I clutched my tablecloth and held it to my nose. I smelled a hint of Ida's house and smiled. *Imagine making such beautiful things—with no hands!* Ida's determination and strength gave me hope. Certainly, my short journey could be no harder than her daily struggles.

I pulled out Papa's shirt and clutched both items tightly to my chest. Having Papa and Ida with me in this way gave me some comfort—the security of something small that remained unchanged. But they were also a reminder of all I longed for. Not only the people we left behind, but my little world as well—the familiar, dreary sameness of Serradifalco. The humdrum little town I had so wanted to escape when I was young was the very thing I now missed.

CHAPTER FOURTEEN

At Sea

By the time the *Patria* reached the Atlantic Ocean, seasickness had swept over the vessel like an angry wave. The cramped, stale sleeping quarters made us queasy at night, but fortunately, during the day, the deck above steerage offered fresh air. We crowded against the railing at the stern of the ship, our legs and shoulders touching those of strangers. I noticed the people on the deck one level above ours. Unobstructed air gently blew through their hair and clothing. A canopy shaded them from the scorching sun. These passengers were not crammed together like we were. They could have danced had they chosen to!

"Mamma, look at them!" I yelled above the wind. "How much cooler it must be up there! It is not fair!"

"We are third-class. They are first."

I continued to stare. "I wish I could go up there, if only for one minute!"

"Well, you cannot. They paid more money for their tickets than we did." She spread her arms, fingers splayed.

By our third night on the *Patria*, the food Mamma had brought was gone, and we ate in the steerage dining room. The long metal tables and benches provided a welcome break from our cabin. The food—herring and potatoes—was not so welcome. This fish was said to prevent seasickness, but the smell alone was enough to turn my insides. I missed our Serradifalco soup. Tasteless as it was, it never made me sick.

After we ate, we returned to our cabin. Mamma sat, hunched over, with her arms crisscrossed over her stomach. She turned to me, white in the dim light of steerage.

"Mamma, what is it?"

"Nothing. I will be fine."

That night, the ocean reeled, its waves slamming so hard into the *Patria*, I swore it would split in half. Mamma retched over the side of her bed into a food tin. The stench in steerage grew, and I held my sleeve over my face. I understood now why Mario hadn't mentioned his voyage. Perhaps he feared that if I knew how awful it was, I would not come. Now of course, it did not matter that I knew. I had begun this journey, and I would finish it.

The next day, Mamma was too weak to get out of bed. "Gaetana, take care of the family." She swallowed. "I cannot."

Such words from my mother! "Mamma, no. You will be well."

"No. The cruel sea makes certain of that."

What if it is more than the sea? Could the doctors in Palermo have missed something? I scrutinized her face, drained of color, her lips

cracked and bleeding. My fingers automatically drifted to my face, as if to be certain mine was not like hers.

"The children, Gaetana."

"Yes, Mamma."

Three days on deck without Mamma. *Will she make it to America? If she does, will they let her in?* All day I ran back and forth to check on her. Each time I became more worried. Despite Mamma's assurances to me that her illness would cease when the ocean calmed, I couldn't shake my feeling of foreboding.

Mia asked me for what seemed like the hundredth time, "Gaetana, still I see no land. When, when, when will we get to America?" *How does Mamma do this?*

"No matter how many times you ask me, the answer is the same. I . . . do . . . not . . . know," I said with measured patience.

"When?" she screamed.

"Soon."

"That is what you said last time!"

"I know, Mia, but this time I mean it." My little sister frowned. I would not have believed me, either.

Mamma, please get better! I longed for the time when I could be just me, rather than *Mamma* and me. But such thoughts no sooner crept into my head than I was overcome with guilt. Poor Mamma was getting weaker by the day! How could I complain?

On our seventh day at sea, Nino talked for one straight hour of how bored he was, and I lost my temper. "Nino!" I shouted. "Go away! Do something. Anything but bother me! Jump over the side of the ship, for all I care!"

"You jump!" he shouted. "We do not need you anyway! We need a man—like me!" He poked his thumb at his chest.

Giggles coming from above drew my eyes to a girl with long brown hair, leaning over the first-class deck railing. A young boy, about Nino's size, stood beside her.

"I have one of those," she said, pointing to Nino with a thrust of her chin.

"Would you like another?" I asked playfully.

"No, thank you," she laughed. "One is more than enough." She started toward the stairs, and the boy grabbed her sleeve.

"Anna, Mamma would not allow you to go down there!"

"Let go of me, Vito!" She pulled her arm from the boy's grasp. "Mamma is not here. She will not know what I do unless you tell her."

"Then I will write to her once we get to America."

"Do it, Vito. I am tired of this boring ship and the boring people who perch up here. I am going down there to talk to that funny girl. And *you* cannot stop me!"

"I *will* stop you! I will write Mamma a letter and tell her how you did not obey her!"

"Only if you want me to announce that last night you wet your . . ."

"No! No, Anna! Please!"

"Well, then . . ." She brushed his hand off her sleeve and came down the stairs to stand before me. She held out her hand. "I am Anna Santo."

Just then, the ship rolled. I lost my balance and staggered forward. My hand brushed her crisp, lacy sleeve. A beautiful ring, with a shiny white stone, encircled her finger.

"My name is Gaetana Curatolo," I said. "They call me Ta."

"Gaetana," Nino interrupted, "No one calls you . . ."

"Quiet, Nino."

"Gaetana," said Anna. "What a pretty name! But I will call you Ta if you wish." She looked at Nino and Mia, and back to me. "I, too, am traveling without my parents."

"No," I answered. "My mother rests below." I introduced Nino and Mia to Anna.

"I travel with my brother, Vito," Anna said. "My mother is in Palermo with my ill sister. They will cross when she is well. And my father is already in America. Oh, I cannot wait to see my papa! Where is *your* father?"

"He is not with us."

"Where is he? In Sicily or America?"

"In Sicily."

Mia piped in. "He is dead."

"Oh!" Anna gasped. She surveyed my black dress. "I am very sorry. I should have known. Oh, I am so very sorry!" She was silent for a moment. I fidgeted with my hair. *She does not want to be friends with a papa-less girl.*

Just then Anna's brother called down to her. "Anna! It is time to eat, and if we do not hurry, we will not have time to change our clothes."

People with fancy clothes and jewelry change their clothes to eat! Despite our obvious differences, I liked the girl and hoped to see her again.

As we made our way down the stairs that evening, I thought of my new friend. Surely we would have something in common besides our loathsome brothers. *I will tell her about Mario. Perhaps she, too, has someone waiting for her across the ocean.*

Thinking of Mario brought a smile to my lips. But it quickly disappeared when I saw Mamma sprawled on her bed.

CHAPTER FIFTEEN

The Stranger

I fell to my knees. "Mamma!" Her pale face glistened with sweat, but her skin felt cold to my touch. If it hadn't been for her distinctive ebony hair, I might have taken her for a stranger.

She raised a trembling finger to point at the children. "Feed them," she whispered, her voice—like her face—devoid of color. She closed her eyes.

"Mamma, do not sleep. Eat. *Drink*."

She touched her stomach. "No. Feed them."

"I will feed them, but first I need to get water for you. Where is your cup?" I patted the mattress but couldn't find it. I reached under the bed. There it was, beside her food tin. With the cup in my left hand, I jerked the tin toward me, and its contents spilled onto my hand. I wiped the vomit on my skirt.

I held the tin toward my brother. "Nino, empty this for Mamma."

"But you said she needed to eat."

"It is not food," I whispered through clenched teeth.

"What is it?"

"Nino, Mamma is sick. Please empty this!"

Finally he understood and stepped back. "Me? Touch *that?*"

"Nino!" I shouted. "Do it! Now!" He disappeared with the tin.

I must have a little of Mamma in me after all. I held the cup in front of Mamma's face. "Did you drink today?" I repeated. I wasn't sure I wanted to hear the answer. She shrugged her shoulders and closed her eyes.

"Mamma, wake up!" I propped up her head. Her eyes fluttered. I held the cup to her lips. She drank a bit. "Good! Now drink a little more. You can do it, Mamma. *Please.*"

I remembered Mamma giving us water to drink when we had fevers. Many times she had said, "The body can live without many things—water is not one of them."

Mamma could die! "Drink!" I begged. But the rest of the water dribbled down her chin, and then she was asleep again. "Mamma, think of the wonderful life waiting for us in America! Little Antonino and Carlo . . . and Lucia's wedding . . . . " She slept.

Nino returned with the empty tin and placed it next to the bed.

"Thank you, Nino. We have to work together. For Mamma," I said.

He nodded. "I knew what to do, Gaetana. I was just . . . just . . . "

"You were scared, Nino."

He looked away.

"Nino, I am 16 years old. I am scared, too. She is our mother after all."

"But I am a boy! A man!"

"Nino, even the big man of the family is still Mamma's little boy." I pulled him close, and he didn't resist.

None of us felt like eating that night, but I made certain everyone drank water. Mia rested on my lap. "Gaetana," she whispered. "I want to sleep with you. I do not want to get Mamma's disease."

I smiled and wished I knew as little as Mia did. Life would be much simpler. "Mamma does not have a disease." *Does she?*

Wedged between my sister and the wall, I was wide-awake when I heard Mamma groan and heave. *What could she have left?* I climbed down from my bunk. I had to get her water and somehow make her drink it. But the water spigot was located on the deck above. There was a steward there during the day. Would he be there at night, too? I paced back and forth.

Mamma twisted in her bed, struggling to remove the money pouch from around her neck. She held the pouch out to me. "Take."

"No." I gently pushed her hands and the pouch away from me.

She pushed back and pressed it into my hand.

"Mamma, no! Not this!" I squeezed the pouch. Such responsibility! *What if someone tears it from my neck? What if I lose it?* Oh, I did not want that pouch. Reluctantly I placed it over my head. By taking it, was I giving up on Mamma? There was only one way to get that pouch back to its rightful owner. "Mamma, I am going to the spigot to get water for you." I turned to leave.

She grabbed my arm with what must have been her last ounce of strength. "Do not make trouble. In the morning . . ."

I knew fate waited for no one. Papa was proof of that. "There will be no trouble." Who could deny a daughter helping her mother? "I will be back in just a few minutes."

Anger broke through her weariness. "Let it be, Gaetana! God's plan will provide."

She was giving up. I was not. I grabbed another cup and turned to walk away.

"Listen to me!" she croaked.

Shaking, I snaked my way past the cabins and their creaking bunks and up the dark stairwell. *If I get caught, will I be sent back to Sicily?* No matter the risk, I could not let Mamma die.

Near the top of the stairs, I tripped and fell forward. I reached for the handrail, but instead gripped what felt like human hair.

A voice called out, "Watch where you are going!"

A guard! No. It was the voice of a girl. My heart hammered in my chest. "Please move!" I stood, groping for the handrail.

We both clambered up the stairs.

She whispered, "What are you doing?"

I could have asked her the same question, but there was no time. "I need water for my mother!" I blinked back tears, trying to remember where I had seen the water spigot. Why couldn't I remember? *What is wrong with me?*

She poked her head around the corner. "I will help you. But we must be quiet."

We stepped from the steerage entrance. In the pale moonlight, I could see but an outline of a girl about my size. We stared at one another for a moment.

"If we time it right, the steward will not see us. Come." Like an angel, she took my hand.

Carefully we crept forward. I heard a creaking noise behind me and looked over my shoulder. Nothing. To my relief, we found the spigot

within a few minutes. I quickly filled the cups, and the stranger pulled me through the dark night back to the steerage entrance. We parted at the bottom of the stairs. I turned around and took a few steps backward. "You . . . you have saved my mother's life," I said in her direction.

"No," her voice came out of the darkness. "*You* saved your mother's life. Now go to her!"

Somehow, as I hurried through the veil of darkness, I managed to keep the water from spilling. I knelt beside Mamma and gently shook her shoulder. She opened her eyes, blinked, and nodded her head. The water trickled into her mouth, and her head fell back. She was asleep once more. I dropped my forehead to the mattress and said a silent prayer.

I climbed into my bunk. My heart returned to a normal rhythm. *If I saw this girl in the daylight, would I recognize her?* I fell into a fitful sleep, wondering how to properly thank this kind, faceless stranger.

CHAPTER SIXTEEN

Closer

Sometime during the night, the sea grew weary and then slept. When the sun came up, Mamma requested bread and more water. Nino looked at Mamma and then at me.

"Will Mamma be well again, Gaetana?"

Before I could answer, Mamma did. "I am better, Nino."

"Then we shall go up on deck!" he announced.

I put my palm to Mamma's forehead. Her color was better, but tired circles hung beneath her eyes. I held out my hands to her. "Mamma?"

"Not yet, Gaetana."

I started to lift the pouch from my neck.

"Not yet, Gaetana," she repeated.

On deck a steamy rain was falling. I closed my eyes and inhaled the cleansing breeze, wiping away the recent memory of the stifling air in steerage. I held my hands out in the rain and ran my fingers through my hair and over my face. I opened my eyes to find Anna under the first-class canopy. She came down the stairs, shielding her face from the rain.

"How is your mother today?" she asked.

"Better. A kind stranger helped me to get water for her last night. Mamma even ate a bit of bread this morning!"

"Wonderful!" exclaimed Anna.

"Yes, it is good. Still, she wants to stay below." I held up the money pouch. "I do not like that she wants me to keep this, as if she has given up."

"She gave it to you because she trusts you. You are in better health than she is right now." Anna leaned in toward me and lowered her voice. "I have an idea." Her eyes sparkled. "We will bring your mother out in this beautiful rain!"

"But, Anna, she is too weak to come up the stairs!"

"Maybe on her own, but with our help, she could do it."

"This way." I took her hand and pulled her toward the steerage entrance.

"Anna!" her brother called. "Where are you going?"

"It is not your concern."

"It is bad enough you talk with the steerage girl. Now you go off with her! What would Mamma say?"

Steerage girl! His words stung.

"Forget about him," said Anna. "Come."

We reached the top of the stairs, and I stopped. "You do not want to go down there, Anna."

She nudged me in reply and descended the stairs behind me.

At the bottom, she grabbed my shoulder. I turned to her. "I am sorry, Anna. We can go back. You do not have to do this!"

With her hand over her mouth, she inhaled sharply. "No, I am fine. Keep going."

We walked on. "There she is." Mamma lay on the mattress, her arm draped across her forehead.

"Gaetana? Why are you back so soon?"

"I want to take you to the fresh air. It will help you to feel better. This is my friend, Anna Santo. She wants to help us."

Mamma looked at Anna. "Child, you do not belong down here."

"Signora Curatolo, please come with us. It will be good for you."

"No. I am too weak."

"Mamma, if you stay down here with the smell and the rocking, you might get sick again. Please."

"Hmmm . . . you might be right. I think if I stay down here another minute, I will not only lose my stomach but my mind as well! Gaetana, get my pins." She dragged her legs over the side of the bunk and raked her fingers through her hair, removing the tangles. In no time, she looked more like herself again, but for the careless bun resting on the back of her head.

"Mamma, you look . . . beautiful."

"A strong word."

"Yes. Beautiful to me. Come."

Together we made our way to the stairs, with Anna and I on either side of Mamma. She stopped to sit on the bottom step, her breath coming with labored effort.

"You can do it, Mamma. Take your time," I said.

After a few minutes, she stood and announced, "I am ready."

With my right hand on the handrail and my left arm locked in

Mamma's, we slowly ascended. With each step, the day illuminated her face a bit more, and the toll our journey had taken on her became alarmingly clear. Once outside, Mamma cupped her hands, and a pool of water collected there. She let the rain wash over her face. "Ahhh . . . "

At the sound of our mother's voice, Nino and Mia turned, wide-eyed. "Mamma!" they squealed. They ran to her and nearly knocked her over with their hugs.

"Careful!" I warned. "Mamma is weak." I patted the deck. "Sit here, Mamma. Rest your head on my lap."

Nino had coaxed Vito halfway down the stairs that connected the third- and first-class decks. They watched as Anna made herself comfortable beside me. When my head lolled back and came to rest on the rail, I realized how tired I was. To rest and not worry—such pleasure! *Thank goodness Mamma is better.* I opened my eyes and looked down at her. *She is pale, thin, and weak, but she is alive.* As if she heard my thoughts, a peaceful smile crept over her face.

I noticed a pair of shiny black shoes before me, and my eyes traveled up the crease of neatly pressed black pants to a crisp white shirt. Vito cleared his throat. "I am sorry for what I said."

I smiled at him. "I forgive you, Vito. Now, will you do something about this little boy—my brother, Nino—who still pesters me?"

Vito grinned and turned to Nino. "How would you like to learn to play the mandolin?" With the word "play" Nino was all Vito's.

Our final days aboard the *Patria* were by far the best of the voyage. The ocean calmed, and with Mamma feeling better, we spent most of our time together on the main deck, enjoying the company of Anna and Vito and playing the card game Briscola. Mia squealed when she and Anna finally scored more points than Nino and I. Vito played his mandolin, and we clapped our hands to his music. Nino asked Mamma to buy one for him in America.

"Of course, Nino. With my first American money, my son will have a mandolin."

CHAPTER SEVENTEEN

In Sight

July 30, 1920, was a day I'll never forget. "Mamma, do you feel that?" I asked.

"I feel nothing," she answered sleepily.

"Exactly. I do not feel the waves anymore!" Over the last day or two, the ocean had become more tranquil. At first I wondered whether I had simply become used to its motion. Now I was sure—it was definitely calmer.

Suddenly, the ship was buzzing with news that we were getting very close to America. The waves lapped at the sides of the vessel and rocked it like a baby in its mother's arms.

"Mamma, we are almost there!" I announced.

"When I see, I believe," said Mamma.

I stood up to get a better view and await Mamma's proof. *Will it look like Palermo?* After two hours, I was ready to give up when I saw several small islands and a large landmass. "See and believe, Mamma!"

I reached down to pull her up. She came off the deck more easily than I expected, and we nearly toppled over. *Will I have to become accustomed to this smaller version of Mamma, or will America fatten her up again?*

With one hand, Mamma squeezed the rail. Her other hand cupped her mouth. "At last," she whispered. The weight of our journey seemed to lift from her. I knew I should have been taking in the miraculous sight over the side of the ship. But in that moment, the miracle before me was more astounding. Mamma looked happy.

A glorious noise rang in my ears as shouts of "America!" swept through the ship. All around me, passengers clapped and cheered and cried.

"Anna!" I threw my voice over my shoulder. But she and Vito had already returned to the first-class deck.

The *Patria* stopped briefly, and uniformed men boarded.

"Who are they, Mamma?" Mia asked. "What are they doing?"

"I remember Lucia's letter," she answered, her face transforming from one of joy to one of worry. "They are looking for illness." One of the men stopped and gave us a cursory look and moved on.

The waters narrowed, and all of the passengers rose to their feet, even those who moments before lay lifeless on the deck. A mass of people stood shoulder to shoulder, as the *Patria* entered New York Harbor. The mist lifted like a curtain to reveal the Statue of Liberty, a gift from the people of France. *When I become an American, she will be a gift for me, too.* Just as Lucia had described, Lady Liberty stood, torch held high, lighting our way. An old man beside me fell to his knees and clasped his hands together. Tears came to my eyes. Mamma smiled as she wiped her eyes with the back of her hand.

"Why do you look happy and sad at the same time?" Mia asked.

"Someday, little daughter, you will understand. Tears come in the extremes—extreme sadness and extreme joy. This is both, Mia. The tears of extreme." How lucky we were to have a chance at a new life.

The ship continued through the harbor. The great, tall buildings of New York stood like sentries, guarding the Promised Land. Never before had I seen a building more than four stories tall, yet these seemed to touch the clouds. The ship docked, but I felt anything but anchored as I floated between my old and new worlds.

Anna stood on the stairs, waving me over to her. I climbed a few steps to meet her. "Ta," she said, "this is it."

My secret name revealed, Mamma jerked her head toward me, her eyebrows scrunched together in a frown. She opened her mouth to say something, but then Nino grabbed her hand. "Come. We must follow Anna and Vito," he said.

Mamma's eyes locked with Anna's before she turned toward my brother. "Nino, we stay here. We will be checked again later," she explained. Mamma, Nino, and Mia bid the Santos farewell and stepped aside so that I could do the same.

"Ta," Anna said, "it is time to say goodbye." By virtue of class, Anna would get off the ship before me. The reality that her new life would begin before mine—just because she had more money—hit me like a cold, driving wind. She looked at me, as if to apologize.

"You are who you are, Anna. Just as I am. You are my friend, and I will never forget you." I thought of Ida and the tablecloth that would always remind me of her. I had nothing of Anna's except a slip of paper with her address written on it. *Can it be that I just met her?* I felt as if

I was losing a part of myself. We hugged, and she walked back to her place on the first-class deck.

◆◆◆

I wedged my way to the railing and cast my eyes over the newest Americans. I watched with envy as Anna ran into the arms of a tall, clean-shaven man. *Her papa.* She turned to me, and I waved. I knew that my reunion would come soon, but I felt as impatient as Mia. "I want to get off this ship, Mamma!" she whined.

Mamma pointed toward a building on an island in the harbor. Lady Liberty stood to its left. "That is Ellis Island. We cannot enter America until we are checked there."

"Checked again? Why?"

"Steerage is not the cleanest place on the ship. They fear we could spread disease in their country. They will check us to make sure we are healthy. And they will check to see that we have enough money to take care of ourselves, too."

I remembered the letters. Mamma was right. Lady Liberty no longer seemed a guaranteed welcome. The inspector gave us our landing cards, to help the inspectors at Ellis Island identify us. We hung them around our necks and left the *Patria* for an open-air barge. We were on our way to Ellis Island.

"Will this boat make you sick, too, Mamma?" asked Mia.

"I hope not."

The barge moved across the harbor, and the giants of New York retreated behind us. We were filled with trepidation as we watched the beautiful, red-brick building loom closer. *Could this be a castle, like the ones Ida and I had read about?*

The barge docked with a thud. Nino dragged the chest and held

Mia's hand. Mamma's clothes hung loosely on her shrunken body, and she folded her hands across her stomach, secretly clutching her skirt. I slipped my arm in hers to help her walk, but she shrugged me off. "I must walk on my own. If you help me, they will think I am not well, and they will make me stay here—or worse." I was happy to see Mamma walk on her own again, but in a way, I was sad, too. *She does not need me anymore.*

A man shouted, "Here, this line!" I did not understand his American words, but his tone and pointing finger made it clear where he wanted us to go. We joined a line of people waiting to enter the castle. We were among the lucky ones who quickly reached the protective canopy that extended from its main doors. The line crept forward. Finally we entered the building. No grand staircase. No regal throne. Just the din of thousands of swarming people shouting in their native languages, bewildered looks on their weary faces. *The* Patria *is not the only ship to come to America today.*

An inspector rifled through our trunk, casting it aside when he was through. Ida's tablecloth hung recklessly over the side. *The only things we bring from our homeland, and he treats them like trash!* I brushed off the tablecloth and carefully placed it back in the chest. We joined a line of people making their way up a staircase in the center of the room. Mamma tripped and nearly fell as people pushed and shoved their way up the stairs.

"Hold me!" Mia cried.

"No, Mia. We are almost there." I had no idea if I spoke the truth. She looked at me blankly, knowing such assurances were not to be trusted.

"Hold me!" she screamed again. It was so hot that my rain-and-sweat-drenched clothes stuck to my skin, but I reached for her anyway.

"No!" Mamma warned. "You must walk by yourself, Mia. They will think there is something wrong with you if Gaetana holds you. And stop crying! Your red eyes will make them think you have the eye disease! People with the eye disease are sent back to where they came from!" Mia immediately stopped crying.

I put my arm around Mia. "It will be over soon. Be a big girl for me. Please." She pouted in reply.

At the top of the stairs stood another inspector, wearing a pale green uniform. His brimmed cap hung mysteriously below his eyebrows. I watched in horror as a young girl in front of us cried when he made a chalk mark on her shoulder. Another uniformed man pulled the screaming child from her mother's arms.

"No!" the mother shrieked. "I will pay you! Please!"

America is cruel!

Mamma stepped forward for her turn. A lump formed in my throat. My pulse throbbed in my ears. The doctor checked her skin and head. Mamma winced in pain when he flipped back her eyelid with the hook-like tool. *We went through this in Palermo. Why again?* Mamma jerked her hands back, causing her skirt to loosen and fall from her waist. She quickly grabbed it again, but not before the doctor noticed. He raised his eyebrows in question. When he was answered with Mamma's silence, he shouted words I could not understand. *We have come so far! Mamma cannot be turned away now!*

Mamma stared at him, pleading with her eyes. "I am not sick!" she shrieked.

He shook his head and tapped the chalk in the palm of his hand.

CHAPTER EIGHTEEN

Questions

Mamma stretched her waistband. "See? Over there I was big. Here I am small."

Can a person be sent back for seasickness? I swore he heard my thoughts when he waved Mamma past him so the rest of us could be checked.

"Is it over? Can we go see Giuseppe and Lucia now?" asked Mia.

"No," Mamma answered. "Not yet."

We were dismissed and pointed in the direction of yet another line. Now that Mamma's near disaster was over, I took notice of Ellis Island's Registry Room, which was bigger than Piazza San Francesco. Its beautiful tiled ceiling arched far above our heads. Red, white, and blue flags lined its large windowed walls. Above us a balcony encircled the room. *Is this what the opera house looks like?*

"Mamma, remember the letters? They will ask us many questions now," I noted.

But the questions would have to wait. Hundreds of people were in line ahead of us. Faces of strangers that I saw nearly every day aboard the *Patria* now offered comforting familiarity. Hearing the dialect from my homeland was like listening to a song. They were like me—confused and afraid—unable to understand the inspectors. Young children, including Nino and Mia, grew ever more restless. We had been unknowingly blessed when the children's screeches had drifted out over the Atlantic. Now their cries bounced off the Registry Room's walls and ceiling and echoed in our ears.

For the next three hours, we inched our way forward. *What is taking so long?* To pass the time, I counted the money in the pouch. We had enough to satisfy the inspectors: We had paid for our passage and still had money for food and train tickets to Rochester.

"Gaetana, I have counted the money myself," Mamma said. "Money is the least of my worries."

We rested our tired bodies on the long wooden benches that served to keep the lines organized. Thankfully Mia fell asleep, her head in my lap. Mamma dozed, too, between our shuffles along the bench. At the end of the line stood those who would decide whether America would be our new home.

Closer and closer, we neared the inspection stations at the end of the Registry Room. A kindly looking woman stood between the inspector and the immigrants. She spoke both our language and another. *American?* She listened to the inspector and then turned to the immigrant at the front of the line. Now I recognized her words! She smiled and placed her hand on the hand of the newcomer. The pounding in my chest eased, her gentle smile as welcome as Zia Teresa's on our last day in Serradifalco. I watched and listened to study for the most important test of my life.

From one older woman: "I come from Palermo."

And from a man: "My name is Francesco Polemi."

The inspector studied the sheet before him. He shrugged his shoulders and spread his hands in confusion.

"No," said the interpreter. She continued to speak to the inspector, but I couldn't understand her words. She turned back to the immigrant. "I am sorry. He thought you said you were *from* Polemi, not that your *name* is Polemi. It is all right."

The inspector dismissed the misunderstanding with a wave of his hand. *How easily they are confused! Thank goodness for the kind interpreter!* A fear of reaching the front of the line gripped me, although in the same moment, I couldn't get there fast enough, afraid I would lose my nerve. The questions and answers continued.

"My name is Anna Bravo."

I recognized the voice at once, and my eyes flew open. I leaned toward Mamma. "That is *her*, Mamma—the one who helped me get water for you!"

"Shhhh, Gaetana," Mamma answered.

Anna Bravo frantically urged the inspector to let her pass. "But, sir, I thought I had enough!" she cried, clutching her money in her hand.

"It is not enough," relayed the interpreter.

"Mamma, we must help her," I whispered.

"We take care of ourselves, Gaetana. She must take care of herself."

"But she helped to take care of *you*. They might send her back to Sicily!"

Mamma shrugged her shoulders.

"How can you act as if it does not matter?"

111

"Because it does not! Not to us!"

I quickly pulled away from her and moved toward Anna. Pressing some of our money into her hand, I said, "Signorina, you dropped this. Here. It is yours." I lowered my voice. "For now."

Mamma gasped. The girl's eyes locked with mine, and I saw her eyes light with understanding. She took the money in her trembling hand. "Ah! There it is! Thank you."

I quickly returned to my place beside Mamma. Her breathing was rapid and shallow, and she wiped her forehead with her sleeve. She did not say a word.

Anna Bravo answered the rest of the inspector's questions and passed behind him. She turned to me, bursting with her secret, and nodded toward the floor where our money now lay. I quickly crouched to pick it up before someone else could, and I looked up just in time to see Anna blow me a kiss. *Anna Bravo. Anna Santo. Anna is a name that has come to mean much to me.*

I stole a sideways glance at Mamma, who stared straight ahead, sweat dripping from her hair to her face. She held out her hand. Resigned, I returned the money pouch.

"Curatolo, Luigia!" the inspector shouted. The weight returned to my stomach.

Mamma glared at me. "Later we will talk of what you have done. For now, behave. Tell the truth. You know where you come from, and you know your name. You have money. That is all that matters." I sensed she was saying this more to herself than to me. She approached the podium with my brother and sister. Mia hid in the folds of Mamma's skirt. Because Nino and Mia were under the age of 16, Mamma answered questions for them. The inspector marked a large

112

sheet of paper spread before him. The interpreter, her soft brown eyes looking into Mamma's, smiled and handed to her a small card with words on it. Mamma read with ease, and we made our first American friend.

When she was through, Mamma told the interpreter, "I have another daughter." The inspector nodded. He glanced at the landing card hanging around my neck and marked his papers.

"What is your name?"

I looked at the interpreter.

"Chiamo?" she asked.

A seemingly easy question. But it is not so easy. Papa, honor takes many shapes, does it not? We traveled here to America as you wanted. And Mamma nearly died. Then the inspector almost sent her back to Sicily! I did what I thought you would do, Papa. I protected my family. This time I was able to protect them. But next time, will I outrun my curse? I gripped my skirt waist. *Papa, forgive me.*

"Chiamo?" the interpreter repeated.

I took a deep breath and focused on her eyes, as if by ignoring the others watching me, my answer would go unnoticed.

"Mi chiamo Anna Curatolo." My name is Anna Curatolo.

CHAPTER NINETEEN

The New Me

The inspector cupped his hand to his ear and leaned forward. "Anna?"

Mamma coughed. I felt her steely gaze. But I willed myself to focus on the moment and push thoughts of her wrath aside. My bravery surprised even me. Or was it boldness? Foolishness?

My interpreter friend waved her hand, as if shooing a fly, and smiled at the inspector. "Yes. Anna. Gaetana. Italian names—you know how they are, sir." When his eyes returned to the manifest spread before him, she transferred that smile to me.

I continued to answer the questions, hoping to get through them before what little food was in my stomach ended up on the floor. "I am 16 years old. I am not married. I am a seamstress." And on it went.

When he was through with me, the inspector stamped his records and shouted, "Dantillo, Maria!"

I stood before the podium, unblinking, until Mamma yanked my sleeve and Maria Dantillo shoved me out of the way. No longer in the spotlight, a cold sweat washed over me. The inspector's questions were over, but Mamma's had not yet begun. She stared at me with an anger in her eyes that I had never before seen. Worse than years ago when I had talked of the dead babies and pleaded with her to change my name.

We fell in line with a group of people heading for the stairs that led from the Registry Room. At the bottom of the staircase, an immigrant could go one of three ways—to Manhattan, to a room to wait for a relative or friend, or to the railroad ferry. I suspected that Mamma wished for a fourth option—a room to leave daughters who dishonor their families.

"Gaetana, I cannot believe—" She cut herself off.

We exchanged our money for American money and purchased train tickets. As we made our way toward the ferry that would take us to the train station, I looked around one last time. People rushed here and there, eager to begin their new life. I would never forget Ellis Island, with its shouting people, strict rules, and long lines. Most of all, I would never forget her unintended gift of my new name. I felt a pang of guilt, which drew my eyes to Mamma.

"Gaetana, how could you?"

"Mamma, I . . ."

"Silence!"

We boarded the ferry. My stomach churned like the water behind the vessel. Mamma's silence tortured me as I outlined my articulate speech to explain what I had done. Such a jumble of feelings! My excitement about shaking my cursed name rivaled the feeling of having disappointed Mamma, Papa, and my grandmother.

"Nino," said Mamma, "take Mia to the front. I need to speak with Gaetana. Alone."

I could almost hear her words before she spoke: *You have finally dishonored Papa's family. You cannot let things be! When will you ever learn? Never!*

"Mamma, please understand . . ." I started.

"Understand? Who knows what they would have done if they knew you lied about your name?"

"Mamma, I am sorry, but . . ."

"After we have come so far, how could you do such a thing?"

"You see what happens! Terrible things, even when I was small. Papa *dying.* Your almost dying and nearly failing the doctor's inspection! How much more could we take? Oh, Mamma, my name is cursed! Will you ever understand?"

"No. I will never understand how a daughter can dismiss tradition as if it means nothing! Your name has honor, Gaetana. Papa's mother—what must she think? And what if the Americans had sent you back?"

"Mamma, please listen. Gaetana and Anna sound alike. What is the difference to those people? To them, it does not matter *who* I am, only *what* I am—good enough to enter their country!"

"The papers might call you Anna, but I never will!"

"I respect that."

"As you respect the money we worked so hard for? You throw it around as if it grows on the olive tree!"

"I had to help the girl. She needed me, as I needed her on the ship."

"You think with your heart, instead of your head!"

"Like Papa." The words were out before I had time to think. Did I say this with pride or with the assertion that I was not like my mother?

"Like Papa? Yes, I suppose you get *that* from Papa. But not the way your mouth spouts like a fountain! You blurted out that other name as if you were so sure that changing your name will change your life." She shook her head.

"I know that a new name and a new start cannot make it worse."

She sighed. Small waves lapped at the sides of the ferry. Birds glided gracefully overhead. How free they were! *Was I free now, too?* With a glimmer of hope, I turned to Mamma. She extended her arms towards me, then quickly withdrew them, as if she'd touched something hot.

"Mamma," I breathed and pulled her quivering hands into mine. She studied me and her hands traveled to my face, nearly taking my breath away. "There is no denying it, Gaetana. I see Papa in your eyes."

A sob caught in my throat.

"A shame you have his nose, too."

"Mamma!" I laughed and put my hands over hers. The weight of the moment, however, was lifted only briefly, for mention of his name settled on my heart like a fog. "I miss him."

"I miss him, too."

My fingers lighted on my bulging skirt waist. "I brought something with me from Serradifalco." I pulled out my father's shirt and held it out to her like a newborn baby.

Mamma's eyes widened. Our fingers touched, Papa's shirt a bridge between Mamma and me. Then she grasped it and drew it to her chest.

I shook my head. "He is far from the eyes, but never far from the heart."

"Ah. A Sicilian truth that is not so true."

I gladly fell into her open arms. Her soft blouse absorbed my tears, and I never wanted to let go. She held me tightly. In that moment, with all the promise America held, I had all that I needed.

Mamma released her grip, but her arms remained locked around my waist. "Thank you, Gaetana."

"Thank you?" Mamma's thoughts seemed as random as Nino's actions when he was a small boy.

"I know what would have become of me if not for you." Her unexpected words hung in the air, and I savored each one. "You took care of our family, Gaetana. You are truly your father's daughter."

What could I say? Tears coursed freely down my cheeks.

The ferry bumped the dock, breaking the magical spell. She held me at arms' length and stared at me for a long moment.

"Remember, Gaetana, I will never call you anything but the name we gave to you 16 years ago."

"Yes, Mamma."

CHAPTER TWENTY

Papa's Promise

Mia circled me. "Did Mamma punish you?"

"It is not your concern, Mia," interjected Mamma.

Nino's eyes shifted from me, to Mamma, and then to me again. Did he sense something had changed between Mamma and me? We stood on the gangway, ready to take our first official steps in America. *Ah, no more inspectors!* But no more interpreters, either.

I scanned the group of waiting welcomers. They spoke words I did not know but understood fully. Their tears and smiles told the stories of those for whom they waited. I knew those tears well. Hopeful, I looked for a familiar face. From our letters, Giuseppe and Lucia knew when we were due to arrive. What if they could not come? *Will we have to travel to Rochester, New York, by ourselves?*

The sight of my waiting family was one I will never forget. "There, Mamma! There they are!" I called, running.

Lucia and Dante stood craning their necks to see the arrivals.

Giuseppe and Caterina, holding their sons, spotted us and waved. And there, behind Giuseppe, stood Mario. My heart pounded in my chest, thrilled that he had come to meet me. At the same time, I almost wished he had not. I suspected that I did not look my best.

We couldn't reach them fast enough. I first went to my brother and stumbled into his embrace. The tears of extreme came then, and they were clearly those of joy. Lucia went from Mamma's arms to my own. And Caterina had her turn as well. Mamma wept and held her younger grandson. "You are so beautiful! Give Nonna a kiss!" Little Antonino peeked out from behind Caterina.

Mario bowed his head and took Mamma's hand. "Welcome to America, Signora Curatolo." He turned to me. I smoothed my skirt and brushed the hair from my eyes, as if it might help. I stole a glance at Mamma, and under her watchful eye, I took a step toward Mario and hugged him. He looked different somehow.

"Gaetana, you have finally come to America!" he said. "You will love it here. I promise!"

"Mario, are you good at keeping your promises?"

"Yes."

I leaned in to whisper in his ear. "Then promise to call me by my new name—Anna."

Honor wears many faces, Papa. The name I chose, Anna, honors those who bore it before me. I might not honor your mother with my name, Papa, but by being brave and strong and kind, I will always honor you.

"Anna?" asked Mario.

"Anna," I repeated. *A good, simple, strong name.* It suited me well. Papa was right. It had taken 16 years, but finally I liked my name. Imagine that.

CHAPTER TWENTY-ONE

Lucky Me

Rochester, New York, 1985

"Grandma? Are you all right?" my granddaughter asks.

I pull a tissue from my sleeve and dab my eyes. She thinks it's funny that I store used tissues in my blouse, but mark my words—someday she'll carry on this tradition. "I'm fine. It's just that remembering brings me right back to that place, that time. That sure is something, isn't it?" I hold up the fabric and turn it over in my hands.

"That was your papa's shirt, wasn't it?" my granddaughter asks softly.

"Yes. Please, take it with you and tuck it in the dirt of his grave."

"I will, Grandma."

"He has been far from my eyes for over 70 years, but he has never been far from my heart. You see, the things that are closest to your heart remain inside it. You cannot see them, and they cannot get away. Will you tell him that for me?"

"I will, Grandma. And I understand why you can't go to Sicily. I'm gonna take lots of pictures. Would it be all right if I show them to you when I come home?"

"Yes. I would like to see them."

"But I don't want to make you cry."

"Well, I might cry, but that's all right. Because those tears will be the—"

"Tears of extreme," we say together.

"Yes—the tears of remembering special people I never saw again," I say. "And tears of the hardship of another lifetime. But also of the joy in coming to the land of great hope, of fulfilling a dream, and of discovering who I really am."

"I already know who *I* am, Grandma. And I am never going to change my name."

I draw her into my arms. "That is good, Anna. Because your name suits you well."

Author's Note

Between 1892 and the early 1920s, more than 12 million immigrants passed through Ellis Island. A Name of Honor *is the story of my grandmother, Gaetana (Anna) Curatolo Giofrida.*

Two burning questions served as the impetus in my writing this book: Why did my grandmother dislike her name enough to change it? And why did she never desire to return to her homeland?

Grandma never spoke to me of her life in Sicily. Regrettably, I never asked either. I was 24 years old when she died, too caught up in my own life to probe into her past and my history. By the time I decided to put her story on paper, she was no longer here to answer my questions.

I have relied on my mother, Gloria Giofrida McAlpin, to provide details about my grandmother's life in Sicily and her early life in America. This was difficult, because according to my mother, Grandma rarely spoke of the hard life that was her childhood. But my mother was able to provide me with the seeds, the facts. Among them: that Grandma was, indeed, the third Gaetana; that her father died when she was eight years old; that she had a close friend who had no hands; that she left Sicily in 1920 with her mother and some of her siblings; and that she did, in fact, change her name before an inspector at Ellis Island.

Knowing my grandmother as I did (she was not only endearing but also superstitious), I have taken creative license. Although the story is based in fact, the manner in which events and dialogue play out is the product of my imagination. I have improvised where I needed to, knowing full well Grandma would not only approve, but would probably be amused as well.

The historic backdrop for A Name of Honor *was gleaned from several wonderful books about the immigrant experience, books about Sicily in particular and Italy in general. I also traveled to Ellis Island—a mini-pilgrimage of sorts—with my parents. There, we listened to recorded descriptions that vividly described the immigrant experience. The pinnacle of my research came about through the privilege of traveling to Sicily with my mother. We toured this beautiful "island in the sun." Gone are the days of oppression and starvation. Visiting Serradifalco, the town in which Grandma and her family lived, was truly the experience of a lifetime.*

The books I read and the "field trips" I took—along with my interviews with our Sicilian tour guide and the staffs of the Ellis Island/Statue of Liberty National Monument and The Mariners' Museum Research Library and Archives—have helped me to create an historically accurate account of the Curatolo family's journey from Serradifalco, Sicily, to the United States of America. Although the trip from Serradifalco to Palermo was only about 50 miles, it would have taken between two and three days, as travelers had to wind along the base of the mountains. As is mentioned in the story, the Curatolos ultimately settled in Rochester, New York, as did many Sicilian/Italian immigrants. Like immigrants of all nationalities, they found comfort in being near those who spoke the same language and held similar traditions.

In the end, I wish I had asked questions of my grandmother to hear firsthand of her trials and tribulations, her smiles and her tears. You see, our ancestors' history is ours as well. To know it is to know ourselves a little bit better. My wish for you, readers, is that you are inspired to seize those stories your families would love to share. They are a treasure.